TI TRY
OF HER
DREAMS

Janice Elliott

Hamlyn Paperbacks

THE COUNTRY OF HER DREAMS
ISBN 0 600 20697 1

First published in Great Britain 1982
by Hodder & Stoughton Ltd
Hamlyn Paperbacks edition 1982

Hamlyn Paperbacks are published by
The Hamlyn Publishing Group Ltd.,
Astronaut House,
Feltham, Middlesex, England.

Reproduced, printed and bound in Great Britain by
Hazell Watson & Viney Ltd, Aylesbury, Bucks

We are getting to the end of visioning
The impossible within this universe,
Such as that better whiles may follow worse,
And that our race may mend by reasoning.

THOMAS HARDY

For Phoebe and Hugh Boyle

Part One

I

The Lambs, in the aeroplane, crossing an Adriatic calm as a blue plate, were on their way – along with several hundred others – to the first, possibly the only international congress of the AA. Nothing at all to do with motoring or alcohol, as everyone was tired of explaining. 'The *Abri des Arts*,' Nicholas had had to tell at least twenty people a day, 'is to be not simply a museum, but a lead-lined underground shelter in which we hope to preserve the best of modern European culture, in the event of a nuclear catastrophe.' His interrogator would usually nod gravely and leave it at that. The current revival of what Joe Porterhouse – slumped across the aisle – would call in this year of 1980: "the nuke shits" had created a climate in which such an idea was not so ridiculous, after all. And their chairman and instigator, Waldemar of Sweden, came via UNO and latterly UNESCO, heavy with respectability and troubled by ulcers.

Mary yawned and looked down at the pad she carried always everywhere, in the capacious, fringed leather shoulder-bag from her student days. She frowned slightly, firmly drew a line across the paragraph she had written and began again in her clear, neat script.

'And then,' she wrote, 'Deborah knocked three times, the door swung open, and she entered the country of her dreams.'

'Tomorrow we could have a picnic,' said Mary Lamb, reaching for a fig and not displeased with any of this: her firm, round, brown arm, the gold bangle against it, the scrubbed, happily loaded table beneath the trellised vine and her friends around it. And her husband, Nicholas – she was certainly pleased with Nicholas.

'Yes, Mrs Ramsay.' Nicholas looked over his spectacles.

'Ramsay?'

Nicholas waved his paperback. 'Woolf.'

'Oh, her.' Mary opened her mouth to ask Nancy Prewitt what she thought of Woolf, then closed it because Nancy would tell her. Instead, Mary split open the fig. Its seeds spilled and the juice ran down her arm. She licked and sucked. It's over-ripe, she thought, like me – ah, well. 'Figs are like flesh,' she said.

'Cannibal.' Nicholas smiled and leaned towards her. She offered him the open vulva of the fig – a private joke none of the others caught, married complicity. Oh, she did love him.

'Come painting tomorrow?'

He shook his head. 'Opening ceremonies. All that.'

Joe Porterhouse, down the table, caught this. He leaned his big bulk across Nancy Prewitt and waved his fork. 'You should get in on this, Maria. You and your books.'

Mary smiled, almost yawned. Poor Nancy looked squashed, sallow, frowned at her peach.

'The *Abri des Arts*? Oh no, I don't think so. Not children's stories. Anyhow, we've got Nancy for the novel, quite apart from the gang who had to pay for their tickets. And I couldn't stand that committeeing. I'll keep house for you all here instead and do some painting or writing. I'm so glad we're in the Pension. The Metropole would have been awful, all trade missions. No backs to their heads.'

'I think they'll find themselves outnumbered this time,' said Nancy Prewitt, and it came out primly as she had not intended. She was fond of and admired Mary Lamb, but there was something about the other woman's happiness, her talent, her husband, the way she had so cheerfully worn, that shut out Nancy. Thin, Nancy grew brittle in the heat; Mary came to full bloom.

Joe Porterhouse called for more wine with American gusto. What was he doing with the British contingent anyhow, thought Nancy? What was he doing here at all, for that matter, in an affair intended to be strictly European? Beyond the trellised terrace there were tables among the trees and the waiters moved between the trees and tables of the Pension du Parc and, as dusk fell, all one could see was their white jackets performing a ritual dance, weaving, winding among the fairy lights: the beauty of the night and the soft air made Nancy clench her fists.

It would be just like Mary Lamb to forget the conference started tomorrow.

'Oh, you'd have been in the Metropole if it weren't for the Rumanians,' offered Hugo Cross, pale man left over from the genocide of the British Council. Forgotten perhaps? In the old days, he and his kind were a necessary totem at every foreign watering hole: soft-handed and voiced, light suited, then suddenly alarmingly fluent in the language of their posting. Just as well here, the brand of Slavic language being beyond the reach of all but the most polyglottous delegates; while the natives, though reputed to handle French and even a little English, had not yet chosen to display their skills. Only the Pension du Parc and the English Tea Room on the front stood as memorials to foreign interest: the first to some former occupaton or brief alliance, the second, it was reputed, to a visit by Edward, Prince of Wales, who had anchored Mrs Simpson in the bay.

'And then,' Hugo Cross continued, 'the French and the Germans got booked in first. Of your lot, I mean. The Rumanians are buying Chinese toys.'

'What I don't understand,' murmured poor Nancy, 'is why we had to come here in the first place? Why you permitted it, Nicholas?'

Nicholas smiled. For some reason Nancy always touched him. 'Oh, I'm only running the British bit, and even that's shaky – Wales is out because they wanted simultaneous translation into Welsh. And there's no one in the world who speaks Serbo-whatever-it-is and Welsh. The Scots came but they're sulking. No, it was instructions from above.'

'Waldemar?' Mary asked, referring to the Chairman. 'I wouldn't have thought it was his sort of place at all. They don't sanitise the loo seats.'

'No, higher than that. Something to do with *détente*. There's a strong faction here wanting to join the Market. Which is flattering but really we're full up – it would be difficult to squeeze even a little one in. On the other hand, there's the big bear to the East and we don't want them to go that way after all these years of relative autonomy. That right, Hugo?' Cross nodded. 'Also there were such scraps about where to meet, more-or-less neutral territory seemed a good idea. Anyway,' Nicholas concluded, 'we've got to be very nice to them. And I'm for bed. What's on tomorrow's menu after the cheering – I've forgotten?'

Hugo Cross took a folded piece of paper from his wallet.

'After the opening ceremony at the Metropole, you split into groups. You'll be in the Palace of Weddings with sculpture.'

'That should be fun.' Nicholas had a straight face but Mary knew better. She looked at Hugo Cross more closely. Perhaps he wasn't as pale as she thought. Was he laughing at them? Did they deserve it?

Walking arm-in-arm up the stairs, she said to Nicholas, 'It really is a dotty idea, isn't it? A European museum in a lead-lined fall-out shelter? Even if they ever *could* agree what to put in it.' She shivered, thinking of her children, Chrissie and Tim. 'I mean there'd be no one to look at it.'

'Posterity,' he said, patting her bottom. An elderly fellow, with rich Turkish moustache and shirt outside his trousers, pressed himself against the wall to let them pass. He smelled of cigars and sandalwood, something foreign. He bowed and Nicholas smiled.

In their room, Mary was slow undressing. She took off her bangles, pressed the mattress and pulled a face.

'But there wouldn't be any,' she said. 'Posterity, I mean.'

Nicholas was lying on the bed under the mosquito net. The old-fashioned air-conditioning creaked. There was a notice over the window urging one in eccentric French not to open it, but Mary did and a moth flew in. Its heavy wings brushed her cheek. They had not switched on the lamp. Nicholas's voice was ghostly.

'A few,' he said lightly. 'Like the Church in the dark ages. Culture would be saved, a little on which to build.'

'You're a romantic.'

'If it did save – anything – I'd be a realist.'

'Art wouldn't be a priority. It would be sciences and the software stuff, so that they could learn how to blow themselves up all over again.' She stood for a while at the window, looking out over the trees and strings of fairy lights towards the ragged palms of the front, the Adriatic fingering the pebbled beach, the shush as it withdrew through the shingle. A motor-bike ripped the furry, warm air, which then closed again behind it. On the promenade Mary could just make out the figure of an elderly man in a Panama, with a stick and perhaps a Turkish moustache, tasting the last of the evening. She had never been here before and yet she knew it. I recognise it, thought Mary, this is the country of my dreams. Below, a solitary figure, Joe Porterhouse, still drinking, saw her and yelled, 'Europe's a museum anyhow.' Mary shut the window. She turned to tell Nicholas something – that she loved him? – but he was already asleep, as remote beneath the net as the effigy of a Crusader on his tomb.

So here they all were – Mary too, after all, for she was curious and it was, quite astonishingly, raining – the delegates to the *Abri des Arts Européens* making their way wetly to the opening ceremony at the Grand Hotel Metropole. No longer grand or metropolitan, but a duchess who'd had her day and kept, in spite of peeling paintwork and rusted balconies, an air.

'The flags,' said Waldemar crossly, shaking himself dry in the cavernous foyer, a tall, ruffled bird, 'they've forgotten the flags!'

'Lovely banners, though,' Mary tried to cheer, but the harassed Swede was already off to complain elsewhere.

'Actually,' said Hugo Cross, suddenly at her elbow, 'the bunting's for the Chinese or the Rumanians. But don't tell Dr Waldemar.'

'How priceless. What do they say? Good thing our Chairman doesn't speak Serbo-whatsit.'

'Well, it's a bit difficult. But something like: welcome to our beautiful brothers who embrace great Chinese toymakers. Almost impossible to translate.' Momentarily they were jostled apart, then Cross was at her side again. 'What it really means is, since their late lamented President died, they've been flirting with the Soviets and dancing with the Chinese and hope to marry neither. That's why you're here.'

'Why?'

But before Cross could answer they were separated and swept into the conference hall that had once been a ballroom. Though not to dance – unless, as Mary thought wryly to herself, you counted the wrangling and elaborate minuet Nicholas told her had gone on behind the scenes on the subject of *placement*. Practically a war, he'd said, with the French coldly shrill, the Italians scrapping operatically even among themselves and the Belgians stolid and immovable as a lump of concrete. 'But do the Belgians have any arts?' Mary had asked. ('Little bits,' he'd said, 'here and there.') Poor Waldemar had been on Valium and still was, popping pills like Smarties.

The atmosphere was humid, the air-conditioning had broken down, the simultaneous translation system had failed to appear and the microphone was wonky. Waldemar on the dais said something short in English. The French sniffed and grumbled. Since it had been decided, finally, that at the opening at least, representatives of both art and country were to flank the Chairman, the platform was packed. It would not have done, apparently, to have a German novelist and a French painter: one had to have on display the leader of each delegation, whatever his art, together with a delegate of each of the arts from every country. So there, for instance, mopping their brows on Parnassus and batting for Britain were Nancy Prewitt for the Novel, looking faint, nice but large, Rosa Treadwell for Sculpture, Simon something-or-other for Non-fiction, an Irish poet and a Scottish flautist, sulking. A few Mary did not recognise; and Nicholas, of course, who could have stood for Non-fiction but had been roped in by the Arts Council as nanny to the British delegation. A wise choice, not only for his unflappability but for his niceness. Everyone liked Nicholas, Mary thought, almost with surprise, for it is unusual in a good marriage to stand back and look at your partner and think: so that's what he's like. It was really the only reason for going to parties, to glance across someone else's shoulder and see your husband.

Am I very simple, Mary mused? To be on the whole happy? In the hot room, beneath the crystal tear-drop chandeliers of another age – not so long ago, still in the air, but extinct – Mary Lamb shivered, feared suddenly, then the chill was past.

On the platform, sagging beneath the weight of representatives almost outnumbering the sponsored delegates (as distinct from official), free-loaders and camp-followers, a speaker for the host country said something long, at the end of each sentence pausing with pride for translation, as though he had laid an egg. Mary yawned and took care not to meet her husband's eye on the platform. Next to her, Joe Porterhouse belched and grumbled and Mary wondered, as Nancy Prewitt had, why the American had come on this spree. They'd met him fifteen, twenty years ago in London at a party and since then he must have attended as a roving reporter for an international press agency every war, large, small, short, sad, every hi-jack scene, earthquake, disaster natural and unnatural. How can he take it, Mary had wondered sometimes? Perhaps he can't – that's why he drinks.

As polite claps of relief marked the end of the host's egg-laying, Mary leant towards Porterhouse and asked him.

'What are you here for, Joe?'

'Sex,' he grinned. 'Give us a fumble.'

Rosa Treadwell, in thonged sandals and sweat-stained smock, flumped herself down under the Pension trees, legs wide apart; large, rough hands, strong enough, one felt, to crack a brick. Not for her the model-making while someone else did the job. She chose her stone from an Italian quarry, nursed it back home and herself, masked against the dust, working sometimes under a fine spray of water, hacked out her images: beautiful, brave, stern and final statements. Of a Treadwell you never said: but what does it mean?

'Phew! Mary Lambsy how did you know?'

'What?'

'Not to come to the Palace of Weddings. The heat! And poor Nancy nearly in tears because Manzarotti – that Eytalian who does ever-so-tiny bronzes – wanted literature microfilmed. I mean, I can't read, but even I could see the difference. A book is a book. And when the wretched survivors crawl from the fall-out shelter books are what they'll want. There won't be any telly, after all. Oh, goodie, peaches.' Rosa bit into the ripe fruit and the juice ran unregarded down her chin. Mary wondered if her friend had a lover at the moment and if so who. Nicholas had observed it might be dangerous to sleep with Rosa – a caress could crack your ribs. She had strong teeth, too.

'So what happened?'

'Nicholas did his best, as ever, but it took Dame Gwendell to sort it out. Hey! Duck! There she is!'

Mary laughed. Rosa always brought out the schoolgirl in her, possibly because they had been at school together. 'I never know whether to wave or curtsy,' she hissed. But the peril passed. Dame Gwendoline Wendell-Foster, wearing, as a ship might carry a spinnaker, a magnificent, flowing, billowing kaftan, spectacles on a ribbon round her neck, spilling papers, dropping books that those in her wake immediately retrieved, made her passage wonderfully beneath the trees, around the tables, into the Pension. Scampering at her heels was Simon Non-fiction.

'What's he after?' Rosa speculated. 'Her biography or her body?'

'Rosa! She's eighty!'

'Still sexy, though. The boys adore her. And you know about her and Waldemar.'

'No, I didn't.'

Rosa groaned. 'You're hopeless, Mary. I don't believe you'd get a shred of gossip if I didn't tell you.'

That's true, Mary thought. How strange. Within the house of her happy marriage, she had regarded herself, when she thought about it, as independent. A female with a mind and reputation of her own, who travelled alone all the more delightfully to meet Nicholas at every journey's end. Gossip – that didn't matter, but have I, she wondered, shut out something? Something that emerges only in my books and dreams? Children's books perhaps, but *The Night-Movers* was banned from some public libraries for frightening children; and it *was* alarming – the idea of your house being turned upside-down and inside-out so in the morning the tables were on the ceiling and the cat was in the oven. And the new one, if it got off the ground – what did Deborah find in the country of her dreams? It might be not very nice.

'I have these dreams,' she said, but Rosa, yelling cheerfully for a drink, did not hear her.

Turning back, Rosa asked, 'So what did *you* do with your afternoon?'

'Nothing much. Walked round the town.' But Mary meant, I am saving that for Nick, I might not tell even him.

'And how was it?'

'Hot.'

There was an official reception at seven o'clock at which most of them got more than a little drunk on the local innocent-looking brew with the kick of ouzo to the head and pernod to the legs. After two thimblefuls, the natives, with their medals on wide-breasted suits and their clickety-clackety gurgling language, grew large as beaming ogres and drove all who could wobble their way there, on to the Metropole balcony. Below, the sea was grey, the sky was grey and a sweet breeze blew from Italy, so seductive across the water. Looking precariously for Nicholas, Mary rested against the balustrade and found a young American-speaking Swede standing on her feet to tell her that he found the Congress so far not at all insightful on account of the fireball effect that might cook their precious objects of art in a lead-lined oven. 'So we have an asymmetric risk profile.'

'Oh dear.'

Behind her, Waldemar, not drinking for his ulcers, was explaining patiently through an interpreter to a double-breasted native that the Congress was, so to speak, an organism that, amoeba-like, must continuously divide itself into smaller contained organisms. Not a true parthenogenesis however, one must not be mistaken, since an agent was present in the form of the organising committee. Two heads taller than anyone else at the party, Waldemar waved his periscope neck in search of his next victim and, fond though she was of Waldemar, Mary turned thankfully to find Hugo Cross at her elbow. Although she was no taller than he, she felt herself to be looking down at him – accustomed perhaps to Nicholas's sandy height. Was that what made Nick such a good administrator, Mary wondered? That though his head was not, like Waldemar's, wreathed in clouds, he was still tall enough to take the long view, to come to objective conclusions, to round up stragglers running for trains, to anticipate and avert disaster. She might have married him, indeed, for that competence, that long sight? Among other adjuncts to happiness, Nicholas and his efficiency and foresight had made their marriage comfortable, it ran smoothly. Once, flicking through his diary to fix a dinner date, Mary had found an odd little rune recurring monthly. At first she had imagined, with a shock that surprised her, that he might have a mistress and these special days were their rendezvous. Only on calmer reflection did she realise that her husband had actually marked down the dates her menstrual periods were due. Mary didn't know whether to laugh or cry and only with difficulty stopped herself confiding in Rosa. Then, for five months or so, they had had another female in the house – a kind of lodger-au pair-cum-secretary and, as does happen so weirdly by one of Nature's tricks, Mary's periods changed to coincide with the younger woman's. Wickedly, she quite enjoyed Nick's initial bemusement at being trapped in a house between two pre-menstrual females. Later, she repented, for she understood that Nicholas's concern with her lunar cycle had been not self-protective, but evidence of love.

Mary, the free woman and traveller who stepped alone on to aeroplanes as one used to board buses, had not wanted to take this journey. She had made excuses about deadlines, family obligations, but the truth was, she had been scared. For the first time in her life she had envisaged planes hi-jacked or falling out of the sky, never seeing her children again; she had a frightful nightmare that Nicholas died and she could not live without him, and woke crying. He was patient and waited out her mood.

Mary shocked herself by wondering acidly if he had foreknowledge of her menopause, noted duly in his diary. If so he was wrong.

'I'm sorry.' Mary set down her glass on the balustrade and gave her attention to Hugo Cross. 'I didn't hear what you said. In a dream. It must be this stuff. However do you cope with it?' How old was he, she wondered vaguely, a little tipsily, in his British Council pale linen suit and blandness to match; they were a species of their own, these cultural remittance men with unlined faces of thirty-five to fifty. Though they had more to do with trade now, she supposed. Pressing the undeliverable upon the unbelieving, making mercantile marriages bound to fail. A mad world, my masters. They iron their faces in the morning and write novels in code at night. 'I still can't think of this as Europe – I mean French butter and Italian cars and scraps about lamb. It's so Balkan – different.'

'You've been here before?'

In dreams, in dreams.

'Only passing. That bit on the left going down the Adriatic to Greece. Someone once told me that was the only way to see Greece for the first time – by ship from Venice.'

At that moment a ship did pass, barely creasing the water, a soundless dark ship. Below, in the gardens of the Metropole, plants steamed after the morning's rain. It was beautiful and there was a fragrance, also a smell of something rotting, as though that breathing abundance had a foul mouth.

Mary picked up her glass and tipped its contents into the vegetation below.

Hugo Cross said, 'I saw you in the town this afternoon.'

'Oh yes. I couldn't face the Palace of Weddings.'

They strolled, or perhaps Cross led her, further along the balcony, away from the crush. Mary fingered the mottled stone and propped her elbows on the balustrade. There, below, was long-lost Nicholas walking the gravelled path between the Dame and Nancy Prewitt, inclining his head to offer an ear first to one, then the other. Several times he nodded, and Mary smiled – he gave the impression of an interpreter between the two women, or a negotiator perhaps: it was well-known the novelist and the Dame did not get on. Mary nearly called to him, but decided not.

'I shouldn't go into the market area alone,' said Hugo Cross quietly.

'Good heavens, why not? I thought it was very interesting. I wasn't mugged. Are the natives hostile?'

'Not by nature. But since the old man went, they've been nervy. Waiting to be raped by one of the big boys.'

'But they've got the Committee, haven't they?'

'Have you ever known any country ruled by a committee?'

'The Soviet Union.'

'Quite. Give me a democracy or a benevolent dictator any time. So, you see, that's why they're glad to have you here. To show the toymakers and their friends that they could choose Europe and NATO. Meanwhile, there are factions, suspicions, a little violence – not too much yet. But if you want to look around, I'll be glad to keep you company. There's a fascinating Byzantine church – the only one.' Mary caught a flicker of irony across his face, and wondered how many countless times Hugo Cross had proposed the Byzantine church to under-occupied wives of a certain age. He, too, was resting on the balustrade and she noticed what beautifully manicured finger-nails he had. Gay? she decided not. Sexlessness – or the appearance of it, at least, was another stamp of his kind. When she was with Rosa on some art-history spree in Florence, Rosa reckoned they hung themselves up in wardrobes at night to drip-dry.

'Yes, thank you,' she said. 'I'd like that.'

It was at that moment that Rosa came thumping up, wearing over her long smock some kind of metal breast-plate that clanked.

'Come on,' she called, 'everyone's going to eat somewhere. Poor Nick's been kidnapped by Prewitt and Gwendell. I say, don't these people have the most marvellously square heads!'

'Where's Waldemar?'

'Gone home to beddy-byes, I expect. With a glass of milk.'

Perhaps that was where Waldemar should have gone because he looked, Mary observed, hideously uncomfortable in the smoky, cave-like restaurant, where some sort of gipsies ululated, and shish-kebab cooked – or, rather, burned – on an open hearth. Joe Porterhouse insisted on dancing with the dancers, Nick seemed miles away, having shed the Dame but clamped still to Nancy Prewitt. Mary tried but failed to catch his eye, to say save me, take me out, home, away, something is wrong since I came to this country, dangerous, out of joint. I have been here before but I don't know what happens next.

In the racket of the restaurant, the smoking charcoal that made her weep, the strong wine, Mary had almost forgotten that Hugo Cross was still at her side and now they were walking along the promenade. It was the most perfect dusk. There was violet over everything: couples solemnly patrolled, entwined, boys in their shirtsleeves, girls on tottering heels, the violet touched them and the older ones nodding on benches. An oily sweet breeze came up from Italy and outside the English Tea Room the deckchairs flapped until it was still again and the drink and the dusk and the downy violet brought Mary to confess. 'I've dreamed for years of this place. This afternoon, when I walked, I knew it. I *knew* it: the streets, where they led, the market, the Tea Room, in which shop to buy these silly sandals. The curve of the main street, upwards and to the right.'

'Déjà-vu?'

'No!' It seemed important, vital, that she should convince him and Mary actually stopped walking, turned and spoke so vehemently that he too had to stop: 'Not in the sense you mean anyway – the mind catching up with the eye. For five years at least I have had this dream. I have arrived here all kinds of ways – by car, by plane, on foot – with family or friends or sometimes alone. Once I was in a coach and it was so dusty and hot on the road. Sometimes it's been summer, or the end of the season, one time it was winter but just grey, not too cold. Not nightmares. Sometimes rather dull. But I always wake up before the end.' Suddenly Mary realised what a fool she was making of herself – they must look like quarrelling lovers. 'I'm sorry,' she said, and walked on. But he wasn't laughing at her, nor did he appear embarrassed.

'Interesting. What does your husband say?'

'I haven't told him. I haven't told anyone. I mean, I may have told him about the dream but not that this was the city. I didn't know myself till I got here. D'you think I'm crazy?'

Hugo Cross took her elbow and steered her towards the end of the promenade and the English Tea Room. He said gently, 'I think it's a pity you don't know the end. Perhaps you'll find it?'

Although the Tea Room was closed, a solitary figure occupied one of the deckchairs, looking out to sea, beating off night insects with cigar and Panama hat.

'Oh look – who's that? I keep seeing him. He's at the Pension and I'm sure I saw him at the party tonight.'

'Ah! Our tame Count – Sandor Dobi. Hungarian. Quite a history. He was of some use to the Old Man in the war, I believe, and our late President turned a blind eye to services he may have rendered elsewhere. He'd sell his grandmother and runs a discreet brothel. Keeps rooms at the Pension, though he doesn't live there. Would you like to meet him?'

Mary shook her head. 'Not just now.' She was beginning to feel the effects of drink, heat, and burned mutton. Two Chinese toymakers passed them, chittering like birds, and bowed their neat little heads. But for the promenade lamps and the fairy lights of the Pension du Parc, it was quite dark now and Mary thought vaguely she should be off somewhere, saving Nicholas from the clutches of the terrible Prewitt. Poor Prewitt.

'Poor Prewitt,' she said. Not to be like Prewitt – how lovely. Hugo Cross was fading as the lights flickered and threatened extinction. Then she had dismissed him and thanked and made promises she might keep about the Byzantine church. Not to worry – the Pension was only across the road, she would go in. But just for the moment Mary wanted to shake off guide-dog Cross and stand there, alone, the soft pads of night on her eyes, tasting the warm air of this other country. Soon the Count would rise from his deckchair, she must go in and take an aspirin, look for Nicholas, hope to find him there and awake and they might make love. She held the whole topography of this city in her head but had, as yet, no idea what would happen there. So now the sea was gone, obliterated; beyond the lamps and fairy lights, in the countryside and among the hills there gathered, moving in on the town, fingering it already, an outer, utter darkness. Mary knew that. She shivered and went in.

2

'Am I complacent?' asked Mary of Rosa, breaking and buttering the dry yesterday's roll she rather liked, because it reminded her of her travels. They had both woken early and, meeting on the stairs, took breakfast together under the trees of the Pension. The city water van sprayed its way along the promenade, laying the dust. Behind it, very slowly, avoiding the spray, came a large black limousine, startling in a city of few cars; though there was traffic: small screaming motorbikes and swaying trams. The limousine could have contained a film star or a member of the Supreme Committee, or a Rumanian. The Chinese toymakers – unlike the mysterious, square-shouldered Rumanians – seemed to prefer to walk, and everywhere you went, in the most unpredictable places it seemed to Mary, these small and cheerful creatures might bob up. Mary rather liked them. 'I mean,' she said, spreading apricot jam, 'having Nicholas. And feeling sorry for Prewitt.'

Rosa, from behind big reflecting sunglasses worn against not sun but hangover, measured her friend.

'A bit. But I shouldn't let it worry you. Everyone adores Nicholas and everyone who knows Prewitt is sorry for her, including Prewitt.' She pulled a face at the goat's milk in the coffee. 'Anyhow, what brought on all this?'

'I miss the children.'

'So you should.'

'No. Suddenly. Badly. I feel superstitious. Walking with my fingers crossed – you know.' Mary smiled, brushed away the thought, the dark bird. 'Middle age, I expect. When one's supposed to settle down, but that's when the questions really begin, isn't it.'

Rosa nodded, flicked a crumb at a small bird hopping between the tables. 'I wonder if that sea's fit to swim in. They hardly ever are. Poor old fish, I suppose they'll die out.' She sighed. 'Time for another war.'

Nicholas came up behind them and put a hand on the shoulder of each woman. Mary looked up for a kiss.

'What were you talking about. Looked solemn?'

'Rosa thinks it's time for a war.'

'Perhaps it is.' He sank into a chair, sipped Mary's coffee from the big, thick, white cup.'

'A war! Nick!'

'This is goat's milk. I mean too small a planet, too many people. You remember Waldemar's paper?'

Mary shook her head. 'I avoid Waldemar's papers.'

'Well, most of it was the usual stuff. Famine among the have-nots leading to scraps with the haves. The existence of nuclear weapons making their use a certainty. Need for internationalism at every level. Hence this Congress.'

'So it's not a joke?' Rosa grinned and lounged back, her big legs straight, braced against the table. Mary noticed she had the most beautiful golden down all the way up from ankle to thigh, like fur. Funny, she thought, people you see all the time, you don't notice.

Nicholas smiled, took off his prescription sunglasses, winced and put them on again. 'No, actually, it is not a joke. But Waldemar's really interesting theory is that the escalation of terrorism – particularly the pointless kind we get nowadays – can be attributed to the fact that it's nearly forty years since we've had a proper global brawl. Our leader, the sad Swede, claims that accounts for football hooliganism too – no outlet, you see.'

Mary shuddered, thought of Tim and Chrissie and knew quite well that Nick was not half as flip as he sounded. That was his trick, his Englishness, that she had seen through after knowing him for twenty minutes, and that had touched, even seduced her. Still did. That he could love her so wonderfully in bed, laugh in bed; that when his father died, he wept; that he could still kiss his grown son. Was that same English bluff true of Hugo Cross, she wondered and could not be sure – he was to her, at least, opaque.

They sat over their half-eaten breakfast, extending so far as they could the best time of day: dusk was lovely but the insects thought so too. Now it was a gentle, milky light, an air almost fresh. A carnation seller, a thin man in plimsolls, shorts and faded shirt, villainous face topped by a greasy beret, tried to push his wagon under the trees of the Pension and was seen off by a waiter, flapping a white cloth as though to scare birds. Abuse was exchanged. The waiter went in. The carnation seller settled himself peacefully in the shade of the Pension trees, rolled a cigarette and pulled his beret over his eyes. The skinny black dog that accompanied him nosed around for scraps, scattering the small grey birds, put up his leg, then flopped into the same pool of shadow and began to lick his balls. Nicholas smiled. Mary laughed. Rosa, observing them both from the other side of the table, remarked, 'Why doesn't anyone write novels about happy marriages?'

Nicholas pondered. 'No tension? Nothing happens?'

'Oh, no,' smiled Mary. 'A lot happens. But nothing anyone else would be interested in.'

Nicholas patted her knee under the table.

'Like people going to the loo, you mean?' said Rosa.

'But *lots* of people go to the loo in novels nowadays. Hadn't you noticed?' Mary said. 'I suppose it's because they've run out of sex. Sometimes there seems to be nothing else.'

Nicholas pushed back his chair and stood. 'Well, I'll go to the loo. Then I shall buy you both a carnation. Then I shall attend a lecture on nuclear fall-out.'

'Why?'

'Well, it's not just *what* we are going to put in our cultural bunker, but *where*. Coming?'

'I'll sit here a bit. Hugo Cross said something about a Byzantine church.'

'Rosa?'

'Might later. Might play truant.'

'Shame!'

'What's Waldemar doing? Oh, there he is.'

'Trotting from one meeting to another, counting his chicks,' said Nicholas. 'At the moment doing a courting crane dance round Gwendell.'

Sure enough, there they were, the attenuated Chairman and the Dame in full sail, making their way from the Pension. Waldemar hopped, skipped, stiffened, put his arms behind his back, through his hair, folded himself in half while Gwendell sailed on.

'So it really is true about them,' breathed Mary. 'What's happened to Simon Non-fiction?'

'Eaten him, probably,' said Rosa.

When Nicholas had left, pausing to buy both of the women a carnation, they sat in silence for a while. It was so beautiful, the sun dropping little fish scales of light into the watery shade. How nice, thought Mary; how far from football hooliganism, Ireland, supermarkets, Arabs and Americans. Then she remembered.

'I still wonder what Joe Porterhouse is doing here?' she asked innocently.

Rosa, a dirty smoker, flicked ash off her yellow cigarette down her smock. She grinned.

'You mean, am I sleeping with him? The answer is, no I am not, though I may yet be driven to it unless you'd lend me Nicholas. There is a distinct shortage here of material.'

'Hugo Cross?'

'Shouldn't think he does.'

'I thought everyone did?'

'Bless you, Mary Lambsy – you're as innocent of virtue as sin.'

Mary saw herself in Rosa's reflecting spectacles. The face presented did appear in expression remarkably clear and pleasant: slightly rounded, naturally olive cheeks, puffed out as cherubs puff trumpeting for God, small chin, wide eyes, curling brown hair she longed to uncurl. How awful, how boring to be as Rosa's spectacles told her she was. And how false. I am a woman who has mad dreams that come true. For years we are as others tell us we are: parents', husband's, children's, friends' reflections. Reflections in mirrors, shop windows, letters, confessions of strangers, book reviews. But at the core, someone? Shall I find her here?

'For instance, I bet you didn't know Nancy Prewitt was a virgin?'

'She's not!'

'Yes, truly,' Rosa nodded. 'I shared a room with her at some awful arts brawl in Harrogate and read her diary. But that's why people tell you things, you see. They think you're above it all. It's like going to church.'

Mary grimaced and pondered. 'Yes, they do.' She remembered and grinned again. 'Do you know, Gwendell herself once told me that she wears elastic support stockings! Don't tell, will you?'

Rosa hooted. 'Hence the caftans! To hide the stockings?'

'Yes!'

'Wonder if Waldemar knows. Or Simon Non-fiction. Or d'you think they just crawl in under the caftan?'

They were behaving as idiots, laughing, crying with laughter, like drunken women. Then Mary sobered abruptly and said, not really asking: 'I wonder if I could ring Chrissie or Tim tonight?'

Rosa set off with a sigh to join Nicholas and the rest in the auditorium of the University. The only truly modern building in the place of any architectural interest at all, it had been something of a wonder twenty years ago but resembled now a vandalised comprehensive. Not an unsuitable setting, Nicholas reflected, to contemplate Armageddon.

As a mere camp-follower, Mary decided to take the day off, to explore further this city of her dreams which seemed, in the morning light, after a nice breakfast with Rosa, no longer so threatening. Not threatening at all. As she shouldered her faithful leather bag, picked up her shawl (there were still, she had found, certain churches below the waistline of the Riviera in which bare head and arms were not permitted), and walked through the lines of tables, carrying her carnation since she had no button-hole, one of the shabby starling waiters with a bloom of verdigris to their plumes, hissed after her: 'Missi. Missi!'

'Missis,' she said firmly, clutching her carnation and turning reluctantly towards the Pension. When it at last appeared – after many hissings and clickings in the entrance lobby, where two elderly ladies of remarkable elegance sat knitting and clacking discreet scandal among wilting feathered plants – finally it was revealed that a message had been delivered by hand for Missi from a person Gross.

'Cross.'

Finally, folded, it was handed over, the piece of paper with small italic hand: *If you would like to see the church I shall be at the English Tea Room at four o'clock. H.C.*

Well, I might, Mary thought, or not. She slipped the paper into her bag, tipped over-generously because she felt cheerful, and walked out under the trees of the Pension, carrying, a little absurdly, her carnation.

In the auditorium of the University, Waldemar's American-speaking Swede informed his audience with the help of visual aids and a Scandinavian question mark at the end of every sentence, that in a nuclear strike it might be taken that saturation attacks of around 200 megatons would be made on major cities? Taking even a scenario of a hopeful twenty-megaton strike the most insightful projection suggests total destruction within a ten kilometre radius? Within twenty kilometres a fatality of half the population? Firestorms? Fall-out over an approximation of 5000 square miles, radiation levels of one thousand rads an hour for many days? I show you these numbers so that you can factor them into the balance? Total breakdown of all centrally sited caring services combined with a preliminary survival advantage for bacteria and lower-order species of the underground?

'What the hell's he talking about?' hissed Rosa to Nicholas.

'Rats.'

'Rats would what?'

'Take over.'

'Good luck to them.' Rosa shifted on the hard auditorium seats and scratched her bottom. 'God! I never thought the end-of-civilisation-as-we-know-it could be boring.'

Nancy Prewitt stared ahead. Uncharacteristically, her eyes glittered. It had struck her suddenly that she might get a novel out of this.

Dame Gwendoline discreetly snapped off her hearing aid and knitted. While basically she was behind Waldemar, she could not help feeling that one heard quite enough of that sort of thing every day of the week at home, without travelling this far to hear it all over again. It was interesting that as one grew older – that is to say, neared death – private apprehension of mortality somehow took the sting from cosmic catastrophe. Selfish, she supposed – but was that not one of the privileges of age? Like not doing the washing-up and getting the best armchair? Feeling that she was beginning to think in interrogatives, like Waldemar's young man, Dame Gwendoline dropped a stitch. Frowning, she picked it up and the arthritis in her fingers gave her a nasty twinge. What was it that poor old Sartre's girl, the de Beauvoir woman, said about the old – all kinds of miserable things in two volumes. Well, Gwendoline was having none of that! As a paid-up member of a Voluntary Euthanasia Society, she would have death come at her bidding, as had life, and lovers – and the many adventures that had made her travel books classics of their kind, bringing her comforts, treats, respect, the right to be sitting here and (if that young fellow went on much longer) the right to be rude. Sharply, the Dame tapped Nancy Prewitt on the knee with her knitting needle. 'The Balkans,' she said, 'are like madness – a state of mind.'

Either the Scandinavian sing-song had lullabied them all to sleep, or the implications were so appalling no one cared to carry it further, but question-time was unusually subdued for such a gathering.

Waldemar rose, creaked on his stork-like legs, unfolded himself, thanked their guest speaker and concluded: 'The

What, I am sure, as comrades in the arts, we may agree –' ('He'll be lucky,' muttered Rosa) – 'but after this morning it must be clear to all of us that of primary importance is the *Where*.'

Rosa stuck her fork into a buffet sardine in the University canteen.

'Another study group for Waldemar to hatch. He does love sub-committees.'

'Well, I think,' said Henri Fourges, for France and Art, '*Moi, je crois* that Paris is the best shelter for our *Abri*.'

'Why won't he speak English properly,' Rosa groaned, 'he knows perfectly well how.'

'But Paris, you see,' said Nicholas, 'is likely to be a first strike target – as is the whole of Europe.'

'Then why we bother?' Manzarotti drowned his small dead fish in olive oil which looked suspiciously like diesel.

'For that very reason.' Nicholas peered glumly at his potato salad. 'It's a pity we can do so little for the performing arts. Music, of course, even instruments, tapes obviously, but neither conductor nor performer. Video tapes, I suppose, as for the theatre and ballet, but there'd be no guarantee they would have the facility for play-back, even if we buried the equipment.'

Rosa saw him put down his fork and leaned across the table. 'Don't you want that potato salad?'

'It's got bits of green in it.'

'Yum.' Rosa, always one of life's better eaters, disposed happily of Nicholas's lunch.

Nancy Prewitt shuddered, stricken by both Rosa's appetite and Nicholas's scenario. 'You mean Europe will be the battlefield?'

'Well, that's for Waldemar and his gang to say, really, but it makes sense. Why mess in your own backyard?'

Poor Nancy nibbled her dry crust. Nicholas's remarks had quite put out of her head the germ of a budding plot that she had perceived in the auditorium when her eyes had glittered with the possibility of conception. Now it was gone – so fragile, these images, whispers, shafts of illumination, blown on the wind. Nancy was only here at all because she had been asked and her publisher had pressed, her agent too. Longingly, she dreamed of her little Hampstead flat, her typewriter and her cat, her indoor plants suspiring in plastic bags on the windowsill. The truth was, that was the only place she felt safe, alive. She refused parties to summon from her imagination parties more wonderful than any she might attend; she had turned down one husband, rejected lovers, yet wrote – the reviewers unfailingly remarked – with an extraordinary perception of the relationships between the sexes. Worlds she could call up without leaving her tidy desk to stamp round the earth like that terrible Gwendell woman. Only in the dark of the night, on the black dog days when the fire burned low, and lately, here, in this threatening, impossible country on such a venture, did Nancy remember Trigorin in *The Seagull*: 'I am eating my own life.'

And now here was the Gwendell itself, helping Waldemar to round everyone up for the afternoon session, to elect a subcommittee to decide where to bury all those words, all that beauty.

Sad, thought Nicholas, padding amiably along beside Gwendell, and pausing with her to look out over the sea – white now under a high sun – how sad to contemplate Rosa's high-striding giants, Nancy's words, those dumb music-sheets of singing notes, buried beneath the earth; and Henri's wild colours, weeping and laughing faces, locked away in some bunker, perhaps for ever, lost.

The Dame was saying at least it was nice to be away from all those strikes and Arabs and street bombs. Something to be said for an authoritarian regime. See how Africa fell apart when the tribal system broke up. One needed to know where one was, which reminded her: where was Mary? The Dame spoke with affection, as though pinning on a medal.

'Oh, pottering, you know,' said Nicholas. 'Finding her way around.'

'Funny country this,' said Gwendell as they watched a man on the beach kick a mule under the two o'clock sun. The mule wore a hat, with holes for the ears. They shimmered, mule and man shook under the light.

'You've been here before?'

'Thirty-six.'

'Has it changed much?'

'Everywhere begins to look like anywhere else, after a time.'

What Mary was actually doing, as her husband and the Dame contemplated all sorts of things, was watching a nice-looking young couple in an outdoor café in the main and only shopping street. Apart from the market, where she had spent a pleasant and unmolested half hour buying copper jewellery that would prove a mistake, and a most beautiful silk scarf that would turn out to be a bargain. (Later, Rosa, with her passion for clanking, would snap up the copper, so it was not wasted, after all.)

This main street, ending in a small square where she now sat drinking something nice, sweet and strange, was – as she knew from her dreams – the place you went for money if you could ever find a time the bank was open, for hairdressing if you were fool enough, for proper jewellery, for clothes with any pretence of chic, for flowers more exotic than the ubiquitous carnation, for bread fresh-baked and for the most dangerous and delicious-looking cakes.

All this Mary recognised from her dreams (a phenomenon that, this good morning, amused rather than disturbed her). But in her dreams, she realised suddenly, there had been few people, sometimes none. Or perhaps there were people and they could not see her? Certainly though, there was none of this smell – hot, foreign and pierced by something sharp – no bustle and honking and yelling of traffic.

The florist's window streamed with water. It was the height of the day's heat but the plane trees gave shelter.

Mary lit a cigarette and smiled with pleasure. Her pad was open on the table but Deborah was still stuck, her hand on the door; Mary had no impulse to write this morning, she wanted rather to relish the sport of street-watching that can only be properly pursued in an outdoor café in a hot country. Observing the young couple – the girl so fair her ash-blonde hair was almost white, the boy dark-haired, head bent, angular, listening – Mary was reminded of Tim and Chrissie, but happily, not with this morning's odd pang; that need to reach them if only on the telephone. The girl caught Mary's glance. She wore a thin gold chain, Mary noticed, at her ankle. They had the same blue-backed guide to the town Mary had seen elsewhere, so they must be tourists. Was the boy trying to get her into bed? Or did he want to go sightseeing while she preferred to stay in the café? She could not tell what language they were speaking. As Mary watched them, one of the raucous, ambulant carnation sellers, big basket on his arm, pushed his way between the tables, blocking her view. He paused to make a sale, to haggle, to screech, appealing apparently, for justice, to agree terms finally with much despair, and, this opera completed, turned to Mary as his next victim. By then, the two at the table had gone and the flower seller had started on Mary.

He began with winning smiles and made as though to thrust the whole basket into her lap.

Mary shook her head. He screeched, he winked, he sighed.

'Angless?'

'*Oui*,' she said, '*anglaise*. But I do not wish to buy your carnations.'

'Pity *fleurs*.'

'Yes, they are very pretty flowers. But I have one already, you see.' So she had, the one Nicholas gave her at breakfast that she had carried round all morning; it lay now on the table, on someone's abandoned newspaper.

The man looked, almost spat. '*Morte*,' he flung at her and her poor little flower, and turned away, resuming his hideous call.

Mary picked up the carnation, her carnation, and thought: yes, it was wilting, you could say it was dead. That man had given her the shivers over one dead flower. Dead. She called the waiter and conveyed that she would like another of the syrupy drinks and something to eat. While she waited, she opened the unreadable newspaper. She could make no sense of it at all – a grounding in Latin was no help here. On the front page was the familiar picture of what appeared to be armed police with their shields, their masks and their tear-gas, a bank, and the smudged shape of figures running away. Glancing without much hope at the text, Mary saw one word she could recognise, and gathered that there had been another bank-raid in Milan. She ate her lunch, sat for a time, then, window-shopping idly, saw in the deep corner of the jeweller's shadowed window a string of yellowy beads. She peered more closely, walked on, then paused and turned back, deciding that if the shop was closed, that was that. Finding it open, she took this also for a sign, and walked in (thinking that there might be for Deborah more than one door? Many she might open before she reached the central room of her dreams, secret even to her). The light was discreet. It might have been Bond Street but for the faint thread of incense or joss stick mingled, behind the scenes, with the smell of Turkish coffee.

No screeching, no haggling this time. The man approached the counter almost tentatively; tall, thin, dressed in undertaker's black with deep, starched cuffs, he laid his white hands on the glass counter as if they, too, might be for sale. A smile and nod, as though he had been expecting her. (*I expected you, Deborah, said the guardian of the first door, and, after all, she was not at all frightened.*)

'Those beads in the corner –' Mary pointed. Whatever was the French for amber? As he lifted them out, laid them on a velvet cloth on the counter, she struggled: '*Combien?*'

'These are amber,' he said in English only slightly accented. 'For the man.'

'I know. I've seen them in Greece. They're called worry beads?'

'Yes.' He paused, making no attempt to sell, as they both considered the pool of resinous amber. 'They are believed also to hold off sickness. They are not for sale. An order for a customer, but I may get you the same.'

'How long?'

He held up his fingers. 'Two weeks? You may find them in other places but not so good. And the price, I believe, is fair.'

'Yes, it is. But we leave in two weeks.'

'Ten days? I can do in ten days.'

Ten days, Mary agreed, yes, and left the shop. Only later did she remember Nicholas had said something about tying things up earlier if they could get anyone to agree about anything, since Waldemar had an African lecture tour on the cultural aspects of politics or the political aspects of culture. That is if Africa would sit still long enough to listen. Dear Waldemar – Mary was very fond of him, and not only because he had introduced her to Nick. Permanently harassed, he remained the only truly good man of power she had ever encountered. Goodness, she thought, where did it go? When did cleverness take over? And charity become a matter not of natural kindness, duty even, but of conscience, of a vague guilt that haunted everyone who had enough to eat and a roof over their heads (and probably a swimming pool or a holiday cottage in the Dordogne) – when did that happen?

At the University, it was agreed that there should be meetings about meetings to appoint a sub-committee for the siting of the underground shelter for the Arts. In fact, everyone knew but no one would dream of saying, Waldemar probably had the whole thing sewn up already, and on their breakfast plates the favoured few would find little notes from the Chairman inviting them to a sub-committee. And no one would dare to attack this procedure as undemocratic for what, above all things, did Waldemar represent but democracy? He had given his life to it and would die for it. Sometimes one felt he had invented it.

It was hot and mad working through the siesta hour. The Dame dropped off, woke up, and counted her stitches aloud.

In the English Tea Room Mary looked for Hugo Cross. He stood and waved and Mary saw that seated opposite him, with his back to her, was a familiar head. She sat by Cross, in a pretty cane chair, and gazed around at the décor of lattice, ferns, white wrought-iron tables, mosaic floor, elaborately framed mirrors.

'What a wonderful place! Like the Tzarina's last afternoon.'

The second man nodded. 'But the balcony, you see – English deckchairs. Very cricket.'

'Oh, very.'

Hugo had been calling the waiter.

'I'm sorry, Mary, I should have said. This is Count Dobi. Dobbins, Mrs Lamb.'

Dobi inclined his head. 'We met on the stairs at the Pension.'

What feeling did he give with his moustache and scent of sandalwood with something oily, his lids drooping at each corner – wisdom? malice? experience? Mary accepted a thick white cup, with one tea-bag and lukewarm water.

'You should have stayed with *citron pressé* or Turkish coffee. The only bad thing here is the English tea.' That is a beautiful scarf, Missis Lamb.'

'I bought it this morning in the market.'

'I could have got it for you wholesale. And now, alas, I must go. I shall see you again, Missis Lamb. This is a small town.'

'What a funny man.' Mary put her tea-bag in the saucer. A woman across from their table was feeding her lap-dog sugar lumps. Hugo Cross's mind had seemed elsewhere and now he turned to her. What was it she had thought about him? Something hurt, secret, secret laughter or pain. He was being nice now, attentive.

'Oh, old Dobbins, yes. One bumps into him everywhere. He's a one-man central bureau of information – knows everything before it's even happened.

Mary accepted a wickedly rich cake. All this place lacked, she thought, was a Palm Court orchestra; perhaps they were waiting in the wings.

'Is he a friend?' As soon as she had spoken she doubted that Hugo Cross had friends. He had that air of a solitary. But he seemed to enjoy gossip, that was something.

'That's interesting,' he answered, as though the matter had never crossed his mind before. 'I believe the Old Man – the President – was his only real friend. These was some bond between the two, of age, history; and they both liked women. Dobbins probably pimped for him. No, he's not my friend in the sense you mean, nor anyone's now.'

'He seemed in a hurry to be off.'

Cross laughed. 'Probably up to something. Or nothing. He loves a mystery.'

Mary left the last of the cake, regretfully. 'What are his politics?'

'Convenience. His own. My guess is he'd like the Committee out and a strong man in. *His* strong man. Could be one of the Committee. Alexis Blok the most likely. I know he feels that Europe – your Europe – doesn't take account enough of the bear across the mountains. Red is not his colour, whatever concessions he made to the Old Man.' Cross smiled. 'But whatever Dobbins has in mind will be intricate, Byzantine, you can be sure of that. Which reminds me – we're off to see a church?'

'Oh, I'm sorry. Yes, of course. I'm ready if you've finished.' Mary shouldered her bag and put on her dark glasses. Cross paid and they walked from the room. 'I've been rude – done nothing but ask questions.'

'Don't worry. That's the effect Dobi has on everyone. You've dropped something.' They paused and Hugo Cross bent to pick up Mary's carnation. 'It's dead, I'm afraid.'

'Yes, it is rather.' But she took it from him and put it in her bag. She realised that she had hardly thought of Nicholas all day. 'The poor souls at the University – I wonder who's killing whom.'

No one was, in fact, killing anyone, for everyone had gone home and most were either gasping on their beds or huddled into groups talking about other groups. Dame Gwendoline and Waldemar were lying companionably together on one bed, though they were not making love, but holding hands.

'How nice,' murmured the Dame, 'not to have to bounce up and down any more.'

Waldemar kissed her cheek.

Rosa swam boldly out to sea and back, to the wonder of the natives. Well how was she to *know*, she said afterwards, that was the sewage outfall?

Now at five thirty, the hour of the promenade had begun. The sea still stared but it was cooler under the straggly palms where Mary walked with Hugo Cross.

She had never dreamed of the church, which was well away from the centre of the town, in a square at the end of ever-narrowing alleys where women flung slops and gossip from the windows, and washing hung on lines across the street; toffee-eyed children begged with a grin, cheekily, but Hugo Cross brushed them off like flies. They danced after them a while, then soon gave up; Hugo was known here for the fact that he spoke the language and for the number of foreign ladies he brought this way.

Mary pulled the shawl from her bag and covered her head. 'How funny,' she said, 'I'd never expected it to be bricks and mortar.'

'Unless they know the period, most people don't. You're disappointed. Wait, though.'

Inside the church it was cold and for a moment Mary was blind, hearing Cross's voice before she could distinguish his face.

'Sixth century,' he said. 'An octagon, as you can see. It's near enough a copy of San Vitale in Ravenna. That was the centre of Byzantine influence. On the Adriatic too, Parenzo and Grado. But you can get all that from the books.' They were standing in the central octagon now and his voice seemed to float upwards to the dome, to blur, to be lost. A small, dark bird flew around inside the dome. Mary felt dizzy. As her eyes adjusted to the light, she began to see, as though the building were forming around her, what appeared to be a circular area behind pillars, an endless blackness, an infinity that disturbed her all the more because within that darkness there seemed almost to stir gaunt and floating figures, mosaics, marble, a richness and a mystery, intricacy and ambivalence, that both drew and alarmed her, so that, standing among the secrets of the ambulatory, she called 'Hugo?'

'Here.' She peered but could not see him and for a shivering moment reminded herself she was a sensible English tourist. His rare dry laugh, more like a cough: 'Here. Can you see me?'

'No.' And now the bird was flying low, almost brushing her face. Mary pulled her shawl tight, held her hands over her shawled hair, as women do against birds; and then he was beside her.

'Sorry. A little acoustic trick. You know – like the whispering gallery. I was in the ambulatory too, but on the far side. It's the dome that does it, I believe. I've frightened you I'm afraid?'

'Oh, no. For a second. Silly. Too much cake and sun.'

'We must get you back to a stiff brandy.'

Outside, Mary kept the shawl over her head as they walked, more briskly this time, back through the alleys.

'Those faces,' she said, 'nothing like your jolly Roman marbles.'

'Byzantium looked East, not West. We're so smug with our European culture we forget that. Their icons were unmatched.' He wore a short-sleeved shirt and his arm brushed hers. 'You're shivering. The dream again?'

'Something.' But now they were out in the sun. Mary smiled, glad of the evening promenaders, the busy street. The street of her dream but peopled now. Perhaps it had just been déjà-vu? She pushed her shawl back in her bag and felt her shoulders cloaked by the balmy evening air. Nicholas would be wondering where she'd got to. Mary turned cheerfully to Hugo Cross. 'I bought some amber this morning.'

3

On the third day they were to have a little holiday – a coach tour organised by their hosts to a mystery destination. 'Not a moment too soon,' sighed Nicholas, 'before the killing starts.' They sat at what had become "their" table under the trees of the Pension. As happens when the first disorientation has passed, territorial claims like this – with whom and where one drank, which waiter was preferred – all these precarious trivia began to take on for foreigners in a strange land the significance almost of hearth and home. Such rights and habits were fragile though, and the deprivation of any could be matter for deep distress that in their normal habitats would seem absurd.

So Gwendell (and Waldemar?) breakfasted in her room, while Nancy Prewitt – the only one without a settled perch – appeared not to breakfast at all. Rosa Treadwell, having given up hope of any other prospect, received Joe Porterhouse in her bed and at her table. While the Lambs sat and waited, like children consoled by the predictable, for the water cart and the carnation seller with his dog. The dog, in a dignified way, had taken to visiting their table for scraps. Nancy Prewitt said that even if not rabid, even if not foreign, dogs carried three thousand communicable diseases.

Mary looked up from her book, as Nicholas sighed.

'You're serious, aren't you? You mean there may really be rows as bad as that? Doesn't Waldemar realise?'

'He realises but will not allow himself to accept. He believes ultimately in human goodness and sense.' Nicholas broke his roll – half for himself, half for the dog. 'Which is why he shames people into behaving sometimes with astonishing altruism.'

'But not this time?'

Nicholas lit one of his thin black cigars – unusual for him before noon.

'Oh, they all accept the principle joyously, then do their best to make it unworkable.'

'It does seem extraordinary. We know most of them, some very well, and as individuals they are more or less rational – why can't they get on together?'

'Artistic nature and human nature apart, it's too big for one thing. Haven't you noticed it's the same with politics? the blah-blah-blah of the big summits, the huffs, the rows over *placements*, round tables, grinning for the press and tearing each other's throats out the next minute. The only constructive meeting is between two people behind closed doors.'

'In bed?'

Nicholas looked up, blinked, but his eyes gleamed. 'Hussy. Have we got time?'

'Half an hour before the coach goes.'

'What would Prewitt say?'

Mary smiled, feeling a little unsteady, as they rose from the table and went indoors. Everyone, she felt sure, knew where they were going and why, and she didn't care. Rosa winked.

The morning was mosquito-free, the bedroom almost cool with its louvred shutters that striped their bodies with gold. Astonishing, thought Mary. Twenty-five years, and still to be seized with such a conjunction of desire, must be extraordinary, wonderful. Rare? She didn't know about that nor care as she smiled down at Nicholas's smoothed face. The bustle and frenzy of her few adventures before Nicholas – how absurd that seemed. Aloud she said, 'Sex is wasted on the young.'

'They have to practise, poor things.'

'I suppose.' Mary showered quickly and came back into the bedroom. 'That reminds me, I never rang Chrissie and Tim. D'you think they're all right?'

'Mm.'

'Wake up. The coach has actually arrived on time. Prewitt's already sitting in it.'

Mary was naked, reaching for her clothes. He still loved to watch her. 'Couldn't we skip it?'

'No. You are an important person. A leader. You will be expected to clap and smile.'

'Clap?'

'Oh, they're laying on some show or native dance or something.'

'No holiday?'

'A change,' she said in her Jean Brodie voice, 'is as good as a rest.'

Nicholas slapped her bottom and got dressed.

Mary decided she would give him the amber worry beads for his birthday, in ten days.

The Lambs were sitting in front of Gwendell and Waldemar. Mary jumped when the Dame tapped her on the shoulder and announced, 'Of course the whole nonsense is attributable to a lack of communication between the British, the Council of Europe and the EEC.'

Mary smiled vaguely.

'Just what we were saying, Gwendoline,' Nicholas put in, his voice firm and serious. 'They came to the same conclusion at the ICA do in May.'

'It is making Waldemar very tired,' the Dame concluded. 'However we are going to get him into shape for Africa, I have no idea. Is this a Leyland coach? How interesting – it must be very old. Someone appears to be following us.'

'The other half of our party?'

'No, a third coach. I do believe it may be the Chinese. Rather nice little people, I find. Such a good thing they are allowed to have culture again.'

As the Gwendell trumpeted on, Mary left her to Nicholas and closed her eyes, knowing that when she opened them, as she did, they would have left the city behind and begun to climb and wind first through small villages and vine-clad terraces, then into a landscape altogether starker. It was not merely that anyone who had travelled in this part of the world might expect these fields of stones and wretched earth – to Mary the topography was so familiar she nearly cried out. That boulder there, the crease of the land, she knew them and felt (like Deborah opening the second door) a shiver of apprehension and the greatest curiosity.

'All right?' Nicholas bent towards her.

'Goose on my grave.'

It was getting very hot.

'Ah, splendid! A race!' cried the Gwendell, as the coachful of Chinese toymakers, honking furiously, overtook them. In each window a little face bobbed and they appeared to be clapping hands. Rosa caught on first and clapped back, then the Chinese were gone, swaying in a cloud of dust. Lastly, overtaking them all, three black limousines with opaque windows, and as long as sharks, sped past. Now their guide and interpreter – an anaemic-looking girl who suffered terriby from coach-sickness – had something to shriek into her microphone.

'We are being overpassed by our friends, the Rumanians and the Chinese toys.'

The Dame shuddered and turned off her hearing aid. The driver shrugged and spat. He drove with one arm round his girl-friend, tweaking from time to time her ample breast. (Just like Forster, thought Nancy Prewitt, *A Room with a View* and the trip to the country with the gods of love. And then – she winced as they thumped over another pot-hole – not at all the same.)

The heat was now so intense most of them dozed, until violently awakened by the brakes being slammed on. They were nose to tail with the Chinese, beyond whom, as the European coach-load gasped and peered, could be seen the black limousines, all halted by a man with a mule and cart. The man pulled, the mule refused. The driver of the first European coach and the second European coach and the Chinese coach got out and shouted at the man who kicked the mule. The guide shrieked: 'We are stayed but the man is pulling his arse.'

'This is absurd,' said the Gwendell and, with her hearing aid still turned off, climbed calmly from the coach, spoke to the man and the mule, and the caravan was once more on its way.

'How did you do it?' asked Mary.

'Tipped him. I'll be passing the hat round. I've met that game before – it's a local sport round here and a reliable source of income. There's only one way to get out – pay up. Can't blame them.'

Nicholas grinned. 'You're a wonder, Gwendell.'

'Oh no, I've just nipped about a bit, you know.'

The remaining half hour of the journey was a lurching dream of heat, from which Mary surfaced once to see on the arid hillside what appeared to be a mirage: a white house of considerable splendour in a sea of greenery – there was even a flash of blue to tease her thirst. She imagined herself to be the only person awake, but Hugo Cross leaned over the aisle to tell her: 'That's Dobbins' little cottage in the country – gift of our late President.'

In the light it seemed to shake, dissolve, then Mary slept again.

In the central square of the tiny hilltop town a dog barked; children, who had been playing round the well, chased a few scrawny hens out of the path of the approaching caravan and yelled for their elders. The town awoke and, like the opening of an opera, the square began to fill. Groaning with exhaustion and relief, the passengers made to alight from the coaches but there seemed to be some hold-up. The door opened but a local in a shiny black suit and open-necked shirt stood, barring their exit. It was the same with both the Congress coaches and the Chinese.

'For heaven's sake, what's happening?' sighed Nancy Prewitt, as all craned to see over the others' shoulders and the guide-interpreter made an excited and seemingly ferocious exchange with the man at the door. This she concluded, then turned to scream into her microphone, 'There is to be no getting down until arrival.'

'But we *have* arrived.' Nancy, feeling faint, was by now nearly hysterical, till Gwendell – the only one to take her seat again – patted the place beside her. 'Sit down, my dear. It never does to fuss until one knows what precisely one is fussing about. Hugo Cross is speaking in her own language to that unfortunate girl and doubtless there will be an explanation.'

Explanation there was. The arrival awaited was not theirs – already accomplished – but that of a welcoming committee. The Europeans stewed in the mid-day heat. The Chinese appeared a little perkier. Perhaps they did not sweat, proposed someone. On the contrary, laid down the Dame, their bodily functions were the same as anyone's – they were simply a patient and cheerful people. Having recovered from that dreadful aberration of the cultural revolution, their natural good nature was restored.

Fond as she was of her, Mary thought sometimes the

Gwendell really was a bit much. She closed her eyes, opened them, and there, miraculously, announced by a piercing trumpeting of brass, the Mayor and company arrived stage left, planted themselves before the coaches and speeches were made. They clapped their own speeches, the Chinese clapped, the Europeans clapped, the corn-crake brass sounded once more, and the passengers were free to alight.

'My God,' gasped Mary, 'it's *Rosenkavalier*. All we want next is singing and dancing.' Then remembered that was what they were going to get. She laughed. She felt better, squeezed Nicholas's hand and jumped from the coach.

'Race you to the loo!' yelled Rosa.

Like an audience that has stepped on stage, the tourists seemed momentarily confused, then Joe Porterhouse, a homing hippo to the waterhole, led the way to the outdoor café's shade and wine. With Nicholas removed from her, along with other delegation leaders, to exchange nods, bows and stiff, fierce little drinks with the welcoming committee, Mary sank into a chair. Joe was booming already. Gwendell had kidnapped a reluctant Prewitt and was talking at her. The Chinese, butterflies reluctant to settle, chittered around the square. Through the window, inside the café, could be seen the Rumanians eating stolidly. Mary wished to be still, she wished to be quiet, in her mind to taste the place as she always did, travelling alone or with Nicholas. In such a company it was difficult. Perhaps after lunch, before this promised entertainment, she might slip off alone. Poor Nick, stuck at the big table between the screech-owl interpreter and the operatic mayor (half-Italian, he looked, half-Greek, and all brigand), Nick who had not even wanted to come, paying smilingly the price of the good committee-man.

'What a sigh.'

Mary turned to find Hugo Cross at the next table. How that man did suddenly appear: fold two shadows together and there he was.

Mary smiled, sipped at her mineral water and thought she might give today's burned sheep a miss. 'Oh no. But it is hot. I've just realised: in an Italian town like this there'd be the sound of water somewhere – a stream, a fountain. This is so dry.'

'Hardly surprising – they've had an eight-month drought up here. No joke.'

'Isn't that awful. When you travel, you see scenery, a picture. A play sometimes. When we got here I said it was like an opera. Then all the time, these are people, not actors, and the most frightful things may be going on. We're such solipsists – at least I have been.' She paused, pulled out a cigarette which Cross lit before she could fumble for her lighter. The kind of man who carries a lighter though he doesn't smoke – now what sort of person would that be? 'It's different for you, of course,' Mary said, asking rather than affirming. 'You live here, so you're on the other side of the veil, so to speak? You belong.' Even as she spoke, Mary was answering herself. Hugo Cross was the most solitary person she had ever met. Not lonely. Solitary.

'One flits between the two,' he murmured with his little smile, and neatly turned the subject. 'This afternoon's do should interest you.'

'Oh yes. The singing and dancing.'

'A bit more than that actually. It's an old Serbian rain-making ceremony. The ritual of the Dodola. All in Frazer, of course, but I've never heard of it performed any more. So their drought is your luck.'

'You mean they're serious?'

'Entirely.'

Wine arrived and lunch. Mary nibbled some bread, drank, and picked at the small, deliciously sweet green grapes. There was a sudden bellow of laughter from the next table and a shriek from Rosa: 'Oh, Porty!' Both were drinking heavily and Joe Porterhouse was at that moment pouring a dribble of wine between Rosa's ample breasts. Shirt open to the waist to reveal a rug of black, curly hair, heavy hammered pendant (cocaine spoon?), stomach flopping above his trousers, Joe might have been Bacchus himself. And as Mary was thinking this – and very slightly disapproving of such a racket, of Rosa and Joe playing like noisy children in someone else's garden – Rosa completed the picture of the Lord of Misrule and Chaos at play by dangling a bunch of grapes above Joe's tipped-back face, then biting off one, sucking it, and he received it in his mouth. The impression was so intensely sensual that Mary gasped before she laughed. And just as she laughed, there was a crack, a rumble like the dry hills threatening.

'Whatever was that? The wrath of God?'

'Thunder.'

'Then it'll rain at last?'

Cross shook his head. 'It does that all summer. Lightning at night, too. They're quite dramatic, these electrical storms, but nothing comes of them.'

'Tell me more about the Dodola.'

'They used to strip a girl, dress her as the Dodola in grass, flowers, anything like that, herbs – then she did some kind of dance, singing and stopping at every house to have a bucket of water poured over her. That was supposed to bring on the rain. Doubt if they do the full treatment today. Frazer's actually got one of the songs. Something like: *We go through the village, the clouds go in the sky . . . They have overtaken us and wetted the corn and the vine.*'

'You know a lot about this. In fact you know a lot about many things?'

That polite pussy-cat smile. 'No credit to me. I had to put together a paper for some visiting American menopausal sorority. And what do you plan to do now? I'm afraid your husband's stuck at high table. Where I must now make my bow.'

Mary reached for her bag and brushed Cross's sleeve. He doesn't like to be touched, she thought, nor does he care to be questioned. Beyond a point.

'Oh, I'll be fine. I'll look round, I think.'

'You've been here before?'

'Before? Oh, the dream. Honestly, I can't remember. I'll have to let you know.'

Two can play pussy, thought Mary, picking up her bag and sunglasses. Mr Pussy Cross.

As she slipped away from the café, Mary felt the back of her neck prickle. The air was charged, giving her a sensation not unlike that which she imagined a cat must endure when its fur is rubbed the wrong way.

Although she lacked a chosen direction, she soon found that that was settled for her by the fact that the village was not merely built on rock, it was of rock: the streets, winding, twisting back on themselves, circling, turned into tunnels lit dimly by breaks in the rock above and by what amounted to landings – natural shelves that hung on the wall of the hill. Here there might be a tangle of greenery, even flowers, but Mary still shuddered as though she were entering a dimness, a mystery. She realised she was climbing with her hands clenched and was reminded of her fleeting panic in the Byzantine church. Here, too, it was a whispering gallery: from within the troglodyte dwellings – so much like caves to enter, though surely they had windows on the face of the rock? – came voices, laughter, echoes, arguments, leading one on to expect that round the next corner the speakers, the whisperers, the singers would appear, but none did. The talking rock hummed, Mary felt herself to be observed and paused for a moment to catch her breath, to decide. Go back? Or go on in the hope of emerging at last? But then she must come down again.

As she stood undecided, not even sure that she could find her way down again, Mary nearly screamed when the humming of the rock swelled, figures appeared at their dim cave doorways, a woman grasped her arm and pointed upwards to a wild green shape, like a tree uprooted, descending upon her, singing and turning, turning and singing. Mary pressed her back against the rock but still was caught up in the wild, circling, singing dance. Girls following the green figure laughed and pulled her in to join them, spinning her around, her hair was tugged, she felt faint, dizzy, the clamour within the rock and its hundred echoes swelled until she felt her head would burst, crack, her mind be spilled.

Then they were out in the square, in the light and, dazed, Mary saw that the turning tree was simply a girl, her hair, her dress, her face, all covered in a tangle of greenery; no goddess nor witch, just a girl, running now from door to door round the square, squealing as she was drenched, at least twice, with buckets of water. The locals roared, the visitors clapped politely, the thunder rumbled once again, and Mary, stumbling and gasping, looked round wildly for Nicholas. It was Joe Porterhouse who caught her arm and Rosa who exclaimed: 'Mary Lambsy, you look as if you'd seen a ghost!'

Mary sipped gratefully whatever it was Rosa put in front of her.

'Not a ghost. Just the Dodola.' She smiled weakly.

'The dance is arriving of the wetting!' screeched the interpreter. At which precise moment, the sky darkened, the mountain groaned with thunder and the rain poured down.

In the coach Mary sat face to the window, turned away, watching the lightning tear at the sky, illuminating the whole landscape. Dobi's villa shone a sickly green. As the rain sheeted down it formed streams and rivulets in the dry earth, the colour of blood. The coach swayed alarmingly on the dangerous track: this morning's Adonis, lips stained with wine, drove one-handed and seemed even more oblivious of his duty and amorous of his girl.

'You've got flowers in your hair.' Nicholas pressed Mary's hand.

'I don't know what happened,' she said. 'Something strange.' She thought it out carefully, as though her answer were important. 'It was like losing one's balance. People must feel the same in an earthquake.' She plucked a few of the little strands of grass and flowers from her hair. 'Silly. I don't usually panic.'

'Speaking of panic, look at Prewitt.'

Poor Nancy, she really did look ill. Mary felt better and thought that was surely rather wicked: to be cheered by the plight of someone worse off than oneself. 'If only we could fix something for her with Simon Non-fiction, now Gwendell's finished with him.'

Nicholas laughed and squeezed her hand tighter.

'What's the joke?'

'Women never cease to astonish me. What were you planning? To put him in her bed? Like a teddy-bear or a hot-water bottle?'

'Something a little more subtle. What d'you mean, about women?'

'Nothing. Nothing at all. I adore them, every one.'

And that was true, thought Mary with surprise. One of the pleasantest and most un-English things about Nick was that he genuinely liked women, enjoyed them, was interested in them not as an inferior sex but as some other form of life with attributes he admired and loved. Even old birds like Gwendell fell off their perches for him. Yet Mary was certain that he was absolutely faithful to her, as she to him.

She sighed, feeling better. It was hard to stay depressed in Nick's company for more than half a minute.

'Go and sit with her.'

'I'd rather stay here.'

'I'm all right now, truly. I might try and sleep.'

When Nicholas had made his way down the bus to the unoccupied seat by Nancy Prewitt, his shoulders hunched, hands grabbing at the luggage rack not to fall as they bounded over yet another pothole, Mary turned her face again to the window. Behind, Joe Porterhouse and Rosa snored happily together. They hit another hole and executed a daring skid. Joe woke briefly, without opening his eyes, to say 'What the hell?' and then slept again. Mary had the feeling of them all riding precariously beneath the darkening sky. It was hard now even to make out the contours of the land and once they thumped and she felt sure they had run over some animal and shivered at the thought of the bleeding creature in their wake. And on they crashed, small evidence of life on a dark road, pursued by storm.

4

The storm, collecting on the way a great wind, did indeed follow them to the town, where that night it uprooted a number of palm trees, carried off a few roofs and knocked out the electricity, before it spent itself at sea.

Mary came back to the little-used, dim and candle-lit dining-room, having failed to get through to her daughter or her son.

'Sounded like geese on the line,' she said. 'Probably Chinese.' She sank down wearily on to the hard dining chair. 'I expect Tim's off somewhere but I'm worried about Chrissie. She's due next month.' Suddenly Mary wondered. 'D'you think they monitor calls?'

'Well, of course they do,' said Gwendell. 'Just as they bug the rooms. One gets used to it.'

'They bug the rooms!' A wild hoot of laughter from Rosa and a grin from Joe.

'I can't imagine,' put in Nancy, 'what they hope to learn from us.' Rosa giggled and Mary kicked her ankle under the table.

'Well, to bed, I think,' said Waldemar. 'A long day for us all. Tomorrow is another day. What do they say? But I have promises to keep and yards to go before I sleep?'

'Miles,' Mary smiled. 'Miles to go.'

'Yes indeed. Many miles. Please forgive me.' He stood stiffly, straightening himself, a correct and gentle heron. What a sweet man, thought Mary.

Just as she and Nicholas too had said their goodnights and turned towards the stairs, Mary paused in the lobby. 'I think I'm too tired to sleep. Could we go out for a bit?'

It had stopped raining now, and they stood, bare-headed on the beach, leaning towards each other for support, as the wind nearly toppled them and rushed on, to enrage the sea that crashed at their feet in wild breakers.

'Mad dogs and Englishmen,' said Nicholas.

Arm-in-arm, heads down against the wind, gasping and laughing, they made their way back, to bed.

At the sub-committee for siting, France, defeated in having the *Abri* to herself, now demanded Switzerland, where all new houses were built with fall-out shelters.

'In Sweden also,' protested Waldemar's American-speaking Swede, 'we have them of the best.'

'Well, I think,' intervened Nancy Prewitt, speaking up bravely in a voice she did not intend to be prim, 'that quite the safest place would be somewhere no one could possibly want or bother to bomb. Like Australia.' Startled by her own initiative, she blushed and sat down.

France walked out and someone called for the delegate from Switzerland. Germany pointed out that there was no delegate from Switzerland.

Waldemar, behind the cover of his handkerchief, switched off the instantaneous-translation earphones and wondered how long it would take this time for accord to be reached. They were already six days into the Congress and due to arrive soon at that point of exhaustion when they would tire of talking and a word here, a word there, would settle the matter. But democracy must be seen to be done, and quite right too. He had felt a little dizzy this morning, and Gwendoline had not wanted him to come. It was nothing though. This climate did not suit him (Africa, looming, even less so) and the truth was that Waldemar, having girdled the earth so often, had lately begun more and more to yearn for his northern skies, for the fresh breath of reason and peace that seemed to him to blow there, ruffling the ice-cold fjords; even that northern night of winter, a fireside – with Gwendoline perhaps on the other side of the hearth?

He sighed. Meanwhile Africa and, even more immediately, France to be pacified in the lunch break.

At the sub-committee for sculpture that afternoon, it was a foregone conclusion that the choice lay between Rosa and Manzarotti. 'You'd never believe it,' gasped Rosa, for once less bounding than usual. 'There was I, being all modest and shy, eyes down – truly! Manzarotti glaring at me fit to kill, while one of those thugs from his Mafia made some interminable speech about the Class Struggle and Political Content and the Marxist Significance of old Rotti's stuff. Marxist! I ask you – those piddling little bronzes. Anyhow, whoever wants to be political? There's quite enough of that as it is.'

'Sweetheart, honey, cool it,' murmured Porterhouse, his arm round Rosa, his hand grasping one of her breasts.

'Oh shut up, Porty.' Rosa slapped his hand, not to be pacified. 'Put me down.'

Mary had listened wide-eyed, just managing not to laugh. All this fuss before they'd even decided where to put their shelter.

'So what happened?'

'Well, the vote's been put off, of course. I think they'll probably settle it by picking a third runner. Like American elections when they're stuck. Probably that Dutchman – Van Doom or whatever his name is – you know, the one who does kinky things to car bumpers. They're so abstract no one knows what they mean so they all pretend. So if he's put up they won't dare not vote for him.'

'Would that upset you?'

Rosa sobered, absently wiping the dribble of ash from her Gauloise into the kangaroo pocket of her smock.

'Not really. You know, you've done something and it's finished and you go on. Or die. You don't think much about posterity or even what they said about you in yesterday's papers. If you're any good. You know that, Mary.'

'Oh, children's books . . .'

'Bloody good children's books.'

Nicholas, looking weary, joined them, took off his sunglasses and rubbed his eyes. Then leaned back, letting out a puff of exhaustion.

'The sub-committee on sub-committees has just decided that at sub-committees we shall dispense with the instantaneous translation – such as it was – and conduct our affairs in English. The French have walked out again. I've never known Waldemar make such a muddle. I really wonder if he's losing his grip. Gwendell says he's taking something terribly strong for his ulcers – masks the symptoms but doesn't cure. That on top of the jabs for Africa.'

'Poor Waldemar.'

'Poor us.'

At the sub-committee for music, the sulking Scottish flautist roused himself enough to punch an Austrian cellist, and was sent home. The man from the *Guardian* was sniffing around and a piece appeared in an airmail edition, several days old, indicating dissension at the Congress: *Cultural Fall-out at Congress for Fall-out Culture*. The Dame raised her eyebrows. The *Guardian* fled on the first plane out.

It was true enough though, a state of affairs reflected both in and outside the meeting halls. In the evenings, diners huddled together by nationality, Waldemar – and to some degree, Nicholas – their only link. The French played violent beach games. The Germans drank too much. Among the British, Gwendell attempted to organise cheerfulness, but failed.

On the ninth evening, everyone found on their plates a revised schedule of cultural sub-committees. Tomorrow, Mary noticed, the final provisional choice for the modern novel was to be made in the English Tea Room. Among the novelists, national delegates, and onlookers, those who had so far indicated their desire to attend were: Prewitt, Gwendell, Henri Fourges, Manzarotti, Nicholas and Rosa. That sounded interesting – she might go along herself. Waldemar was to be in the chair.

'It's sad, isn't it,' she said to Nicholas as they sat yawning under the trees, watching the lights of a cruise-ship on its way from Venice or Brindisi to the Aegean. 'Art should be some sort of international language but we're scrapping like farmers about lambs and apples and butter mountains. I don't like to think it's just another marketplace.'

Nicholas nodded. 'I've seen it so often. Don't worry: at the eleventh hour it will all be settled, as if by magic.' He laid his hand over hers. 'Tomorrow night, we'll sneak off, shall we? By ourselves?'

'That would be lovely.'

A small group of Chinese had been dining also at the Pension du Parc, and now they were leaving; twittering and smiling beneath the fairy lights, going home to their toys. Mary was sorry to see them go: somehow they had become, for her, kindly fairies, good spirits, harbingers of joy.

Going to bed, the Lambs had one of those odd little fallings-out that characterise even the best of marriages. Not a quarrel – for Nicholas would never quarrel, which made Mary angrier, always. Their daughter, Chrissie, was mentioned. Mary was worried about her. Nicholas was not. Mary had a headache and could find no aspirin. Nicholas was exhausted and would have slept. The very qualities that made them such a well-complemented match – his equability and reason, her instinct – in a disagreement would lock horns. Normally they made up quickly and sometimes rapturously, but tonight Nicholas had fallen asleep while Mary was in the shower. She felt angry, then deprived, then penitent. That night she slept badly. She dreamed of Dobi and the Byzantine church and the ceremony of the Dodola, all mixed up with the storm in the mountain village. Mary woke, sweating, sure that she heard thunder. Or was it her dream? She reached for the comfort of Nicholas and he grunted gently, still in his sleep.

In the morning Mary found the other side of the bed empty, and only Rosa still breakfasting on her fifth Gauloise of the day. Rosa, Mary thought, is a very good reason for giving up smoking. She sat down and thought, this is Nick's birthday. She felt not unpleasantly insubstantial after her bad night.

'I took a pill. Where's everyone gone?'

'Fighting it out in the English Tea Room.'

'You're not going after all?'

Rosa grinned. 'Well, as you know, the novel's not really my *tasse*. I can't read. Then we all know it'll be Prewitt. And I suddenly remembered a man I had to see about some marble.'

'Coward.'

'What about you?'

'I was going. But it's Nick's birthday. I've got to pick up his present. I've only just realised.'

'Birthday? Then we can have a whoopee tonight!'

'Actually, we were going to sneak off.'

'You two are the most obscenely happily married pair I've ever met.' Rosa puffed, stood. 'See you later then, at the Tea Room? We might even have tea.'

'I've tried it. Not for me.'

Rosa hoisted from under the table her carry-all – about the size of a feeding-bag for a shire horse – and stomped off.

Mary stayed for a while. With her second cup of cold coffee, she sat on, sad but not disconsolate that she had missed Nick. Restless though. Too tired for action and febrile with inaction. For half an hour she tried to write, but could get no further. *And Deborah said I know this place but not what will happen to me here.*

She walked through the town, the streets of her dreams, past the Tea Room on the front, to the market and back to the restaurant table from which she had seen the blonde girl and dark-haired boy. And Dobi. It was like waking in the night and returning to a dream one has momentarily left, to have a drink at the same table where the carnation seller had plagued her. (Today it was a boy with small birds in bamboo cages. Linnets, Mary thought, and would have bought one just to set it free. But Hugo Cross had told her, their wings are clipped, they cannot fly.) And in the same dream Mary pushed open the jeweller's door and was discreetly over-charged for a string of amber that was, nevertheless, exceptionally beautiful. How extraordinary, she thought, that a mere fossilised resin should have such a feeling of life about it; not the easy glitter of a precious stone but a consoling golden warmth. She could understand how it had become an amulet. Letting it slip through her fingers, she handed it back, almost reluctantly, for the jeweller to wrap and then, at that moment of handing back the amber, Mary shivered as though in allowing the warmth to be withdrawn, even momentarily, she had surrendered those few minutes of her own life and fortune. And yet, how could that be, when she had been perfectly happy without the amber, before she had even known that she would come to this shop and buy the amber? Or had she always known, in her dream, that she would be standing in this shop, a well-dressed English woman reaching into her bag for money, passing it across the counter, murmuring yes, the beads were beautiful, they were remarkably fine and unflawed beads – all this, and then suddenly to be struck by some terrible intimation that made her tremble, made her want to snatch the beads and run? Or faint? Was she going to faint?

Nothing. Nonsense. Goose on my grave.

'They are for my husband,' she said. 'For his birthday. It is his birthday today.'

Out in the sun, amber in her bag, loitering in the market Hugo Cross had forbidden her, then turning back on her tracks towards the sea, pausing for a coffee, Mary recovered herself. It had been the sleeping pill. She should have had the coffee earlier. She should not have skipped lunch. It had been the silly argument last night. Suddenly, Mary could not wait to see Nicholas, to make up, to give him her present, to see his delight. She walked faster towards the front, then, on the shady side of the street, began almost to run, then on the sunny side, weaving her way, pushing and frustrated by the unusual amount of traffic that blocked the streets leading to the front, the horns, the shouting, then a press of pedestrians too and the scream of a siren.

Just as Mary finally broke through and could see the promenade and the absurd minarets of the English Tea House, there was something odd. The promenade quite empty but for a few figures she took to be soldiers or police, and someone shouting her name, Rosa running to meet her across the empty space before the Tea Room, she seemed to be running for ever out of the sun, the sea-light, either laughing or crying, calling, face tear-streaked, then openly weeping as she flung her arms round Mary: 'Oh Mary, oh love, it's awful, something awful has happened!'

Something had happened. It was confused. The modern

novel and its acolytes, including Nicholas, had been taken hostage in the English Tea Room.

'Oh, don't be absurd!' Mary's first reaction was laughter, abruptly cut off. Everyone was very nice. 'Thank you,' said Mary, dazed, and 'thank you. No, thank you. Thank you. *Merci bien. Merci.*'

Mercy, she felt she should be crying, yelling, ululating at the bland sky. But she sat where she was put – in the police station, she supposed – very English, stiff, pale, on the hard chair, while the policemen or soldiers, or whatever they were, came and went, shouted into telephones, talked to her in their impossible French and English she could not understand, except that she understood someone was being fetched to talk to her in English. And then she felt sick and Rosa said, 'Shove your head between your knees.' Not sick, dizzy, she felt better now and Rosa was yelling at them. She wished, from a great distance, that Rosa wouldn't yell. Now Rosa was saying something about going, leaving, couldn't they see Madame was shocked, she must rest, Madame knew nothing about *le hi-jack*.

They were bumping along a back-street route, not by the front, in a taxi. The driver had a photograph of his family stuck just above the dashboard, also a crucifix and a single carnation in a flower holder. In the mirror, Mary could see his face – a little lardy, joweled, tired – a face that expected not very much. She could see him going home to the woman in the photograph, sitting down to eat, falling asleep in his chair as he did every night of his life; and on Saturday evenings they would walk on the promenade, once a year he would take them all out for the day in his taxi.

Probably it was not like that at all, but the idea of this man and his life appeared to Mary as though she were gazing into a window at a vision of wonderful ordinariness.

At the Pension du Parc they stepped from the cab. Rosa paid the driver. Mary stood still on the pavement, like an obedient child waiting to be told what to do. Rosa wanted her to go upstairs to her room. No. Not her room – Rosa's room. Mary sat in the wicker chair, her shoulder-bag in her lap. The louvred shutters were closed against the afternoon sun. This room – except for the single bed – was exactly the same as the Lambs', but the other way round, as though seen in a mirror. Rosa took a bottle from the wardrobe: 'Last thing you should have for shock, but no good old British tea, I'm afraid.'

Mary swallowed the Scotch and gagged but on the second gulp she felt better: now there was only a slight tremble in her hands.

'I'm terribly sorry. I don't quite understand what happened.'

Rosa too was drinking, from a paper cup. She sat on the edge of the bed and Mary was absurdly reminded of dormitory feasts at school.

'Well. I'd got to the Tea Room to meet you and there was someone – no, two people, I think – in the door. They had their backs to me. No masks or anything. One was a girl, I know, because she had long fair hair. Then Nick, I think, yelled to me to get back, run, and I realised it was a hold-up. It was crazy, like a film. I started running – about six got away through the kitchen – then I saw you.'

'What were the police talking about? It was so confused.'

'They just kept saying hi-jack. Can you hi-jack a room? I thought it had to be something moving, like a plane or a train? They're clearly scared stiff themselves.' Suddenly the tears were rolling again down Rosa's cheeks. 'Oh, Mary, I'm so sorry. You and Nick.' Rosa sniffed and pulled a dirty handkerchief from the pocket of her smock, looking exactly as she had thirty years ago when the school hamster had to be put down. 'Though it'll be all right, of course! They simply have to find out who these people are and what they want and give it to them.'

Mary didn't say that things did not always work like that any more. Even in England seiges had lost their humdrum predictability. People got hurt. Governments had either hardened their attitudes or perpetrated bungles like that American nonsense in Teheran. Everywhere, except perhaps for Ireland, motives were often farcically obscure. It was as though violence, without even a name to shout, sprang now like the army of Cadmus from the earth. And who had sown the dragon's teeth?

And then she thought: whatever am I doing speculating so calmly, as if none of this had anything to do with me? Ever since I grasped what had happened, I have been at such a strange distance, watching myself behave quite well. Rosa has done the weeping for me. Look! How clever I am, lighting a cigarette with steady hand.

'You say the girl was a blonde?'

'Yes. Very fair. Almost white. You know, I didn't see her face, but there was something. Damn, I can't remember.'

'Don't try, then you will. Was Joe there?'

'No, thank God. He's an idiot but I wouldn't have that happen to him. He didn't want to come to the marble place but he went off somewhere. Sniffing around, I suppose. He *is* a journalist, not that you'd notice.' Rosa flopped back on the bed. 'Oh, Mary Lamb, what do we do now?'

'Wait. Or at least I do, of course. That's the end of the Congress.'

Rosa nodded. 'Funny, isn't it, in an awful way – there we all were, fighting like dogs, and then something *real* happens.'

'I can't stay here,' Mary said. 'I ought to be there, in case.' She snatched up her bag and, with Rosa protesting behind her, ran down the stairs and into the lobby. The staff were gathered round a blinking television set that showed the English Tea Room apparently under water. The knitting ladies among the ferns were positively crackling with gossip. In the doorway Mary nearly collided with Hugo Cross.

'There's no point,' he said. 'Nothing you can do.'

They sat at the table under the trees and miraculously Cross procured, with a quick exchange in the clickety-clackety language, almost English tea. Bags, of course. The water, hot not boiling, came in a jug and one poured it over the bag in the cup. Mary couldn't swallow it. That seemed a pity. Rosa went back indoors to watch the television. Mary irrationally resented Cross; for the way he sprang from the woodwork, for his seeming omniscience, for the fact that he was not Nick and was sitting here telling her, calmly, quietly, there was nothing she could do. Then one of his silences, so she was forced to ask the questions.

'What about the government?'

'Dodgy. Not fabled for its upright stance against terrorism. You remember those rumours in the Seventies that they sheltered Carlos – the Americans made official squawks. The fact remains that it's a left-wing country, by which I do not mean a British Labour government. On the other hand, the Committee's flirting with Europe.'

'Then surely they'll *do* something?'

He shrugged. 'Yes, it might be clever of them to appear to do something. But what can they do but wring their hands – for the moment, at least?'

Mary sagged. What extraordinarily pale eyes he had, Mr Pussycat. And what a queer and irrelevant thought that was. 'This all sounds very – cold.'

'Politics is the art of the pragmatic.' He was beating an odd little melody with his spoon on the saucer, unaware of doing it; but he stopped, looked up, momentarily held her gaze, then glanced away. 'I used to believe otherwise.'

'But people. I don't understand. You must believe. People!'

He seemed to come back to himself, from a distance. That smile.

'Ah yes. Faith would do very nicely without people.'

'But if they should be hurt? The hostages?'

'That might suit certain factions in the Committee very well. They could not be blamed, and the West would be alerted to the danger from the East, the need for a strong man again. Or that's my simple view.'

'I don't believe there is anything simple about you.' Mary spoke less harshly than she might have, remembering her intuition once, that Cross had at some time, in some way she could not grasp, been hurt, or injured himself.

Then Rosa came out and sat down heavily. She shook her head. 'Nothing new. Joe rang. He says there seem to be two, though there may be more. The usual weapons – automatics, grenades, a sub-machine gun, no one's certain.'

'What do they want?'

'They haven't said. It can't be food, anyway. They can stuff themselves silly on cake.'

Rosa's hands were shaking. She too was clearly on a brittle edge. Hugo Cross left to offer his services as interpreter.

'My fate,' he smiled and did not take Mary's hand but made a strange little old-fashioned bow. Dully, they watched him walk away into the dusk.

The panic, the exhaustion, the queer conversation with Hugo Cross, the terror for Nick – all conspired to make Mary feel that in this, the country of her dreams, she was now lost, chartless. Shadows slouched from the mountains, swallowing sea and earth and sky. At the centre of some great intricacy she might cry for help and her voice, muffled, distorted, would be returned to her.

At last she was alone in her room. Then she remembered yesterday's quarrel with Nick and wondered if she would ever have the chance to repair it. She reached into her bag for cigarettes and her fingers touched the amber beads. Only then did she cry, first sitting on the edge of the bed, her arms tight across her stomach, then on the floor, pressing her face against the wall, rocking, terrible aching sobs, painful, ugly. While the amber slipped through her fingers and lay at her feet. Worry beads. A warm and useless pool, poor amulet.

Part Two

5

When it first happened, someone actually laughed (a male voice, high-pitched: Simon Non-fiction?). Well, reflected Nicholas, shifting his weight uncomfortably from one haunch to the other, that was understandable: there was something theatrical about the moment they burst in – one from the terrace, one from the street door – something *unreal*, as if actors had stepped from the stage to move threateningly among the audience.

He mentioned this to Waldemar – also on the floor with his back to the wall – who pondered, then remarked in his light, singing voice, 'It would depend, of course, how real we were in the first place?' Once fastened upon an idea, whatever his circumstances – at the moment perilous – Waldemar would turn it gently inside-out and upside-down until he decided what it was made of. He took off his half-spectacles and wiped them. 'To our hosts our little preoccupations must look like fantasies of no more importance than feathers.'

'Why do they bother with us then?'

'Because we are currency, I imagine. They take us to be of worth in our own world and so coin to be exchanged. It is interesting, is it not, this business of fantasy and reality – both are value judgments.'

Nicholas kept a straight face. 'You mean it could be fantasy that we are held hostage?'

'Alas, no. There are a few absolutes and this appears to be one of them.' He let out a sigh, a little puff of despair.

In a few hours, all felt, they would surely be released. An unreasonable optimism, Nicholas realised, and now began to wonder uneasily if they were reacting as do so many in extremity: believing that they alone are exempt. From accident, from pain. From death.

Was she death – the scowling blonde girl crouched to spring in the corner, rifle across knee, webbing belt hung with grenades? No older than Chrissie, this picture one had seen so often on the telly, in the papers, then turned the page, wagged one's head and switched channels.

Or the dark boy, who seemed to be led by the girl? If she said death, would he deliver it? It was she who had nodded and he who obeyed, almost politely indicating with a thrust of his weapon that they must all sit down, on the floor, backs to the wall. Gwendell had opened her mouth to protest, shut it, sat down and said, 'I protest!' Waldemar patted her hand. On the other side of Nicholas, Prewitt sat, very stiff, back straight, eyes wide.

That must have been five – six? – hours ago. It was dusk now and only in the last half hour had the hostages begun to talk among themselves, first tentatively, like children whispering in class, one eye on teacher, then, since this was apparently permitted, more freely. On the other hand, Waldemar was allowed to wipe his spectacles but when Henri Fourges reached into his playshirt pocket for cigarettes, the girl turned on him like a cat and Fourges withdrew his hand quickly. The girl moved in on him and he flinched, expecting a blow. She spat in his face. It was then that they all began, truly, to grasp their predicament, to fear.

When they burst in and someone laughed, Waldemar had tried to speak to them, but while the boy herded the terrified waiters out through the kitchen door, locking it behind them, the girl shouted (quite needlessly in the space of the small Tea Room), 'No talking! Shut up!'

Now, with everyone tensed after the incident with Fourges, Waldemar tried again, addressing the girl with an almost ridiculous courtesy. 'Could you tell us, please, why we are held here?'

Again, shrilly, the girl answered, 'No questions! You are capitalist pigs.' The accent, Nicholas thought, was faintly German.

'Of no importance, I assure you.'

'We know who you are.'

'Then you will realise that our survival is of very little value to anyone but ourselves.' Waldemar's tone was gentle, reasonable, almost as though he were debating an academic point with a wayward student. Nicholas guessed what he was up to: establish communication, get them talking, reduce the element of confrontation. It seemed to be working – the girl had very slightly dropped her guard, her tone was less strident, she appeared even to be listening as Waldemar talked on: just a small cultural meeting, perhaps there had been a mistake? Nicholas held his breath and prayed that no one would chip in and at that moment the burly Manzarotti leaped for the other terrorist. Before the boy could even raise his rifle, the girl was across the room, bringing down Manzarotti with a blow from the butt of her weapon on the back of the head. Nancy Prewitt screamed and the girl whirled to slap her face.

Manzarotti groaned, rubbed his head and shuffled back on his haunches to his place by the wall.

Night and darkness. Still no sign from outside, though the girl – Helga, the boy called her – had spoken on the kitchen telephone. Dictating terms perhaps? Nicholas half-dozed, dreamed, reached for Mary and woke with a start. A hand was on his sleeve.

Nancy Prewitt whispered, 'I've *got* to go to the loo.'

Sullenly, the girl nodded, and a bucket was brought from the kitchen and put behind one of the pretty white latticed screens. In turn, the hostages made use of it. Halfway through it was taken to the kitchen, emptied and returned. In the course of the night a few slept briefly but only the Dame soundly – she who had slept on camels, Alps and the desert floor.

Nicholas smiled to himself. I must remember, he thought, to tell Mary that Gwendell snores.

6

In the night, Rosa had tapped on Mary's door and the two sat out the hours of darkness on Mary's bed.

'D'you want a pill? I'd wake you if we heard anything.'

Mary shook her head. 'I want to be awake. It's silly. I feel I must. Where's Joe?'

'Prowling.'

'Why are we whispering?'

'Like school. D'you remember?'

Rosa went to fetch her cigarettes. They put the ashtray on the bed inside the mosquito net.

'Mary had a little lamb. You said that when we got married.'

'Oh love. Don't.'

'It's funny the things you think of. Little scraps. Disconnected. School – you were banned from playing hockey because you broke someone's leg. You were staying with us in Sussex when Chrissie was born and the contractions started. You nearly passed out. The ambulance men thought it was you and tried to cart you off. I don't think I'd better tell Chrissie, do you? With the baby and the shock.' Mary sat up, suddenly realising: 'It'll be in the papers, won't it. Tomorrow. I *must* ring her before she reads it.'

'Lovey, you can't. Even if you could get through it's night-time there too.'

Mary sank back. 'Of course. Silly.'

'Shall we have a drink?'

'No. You go ahead. It's in the wardrobe.'

Rosa slid from under the net, rummaged and brought back the whisky bottle. She slapped a mosquito that had followed her in and settled on her thigh. She drank from the bottle, pulling a face, then put it down again.

'You're right. It doesn't help.'

'You know Waldemar introduced us?'

'Us?'

'Nick and me. When I was working for that publisher and

there was a do for one of those American novels you can use for door-stops. He was sick on my feet and I can't even remember his name. The novelist, I mean. Nick helped me wipe up. And then it all seemed funny. When d'you think we'll hear something?'

'When Joe gets back – if he does. Or creepy Cross.'

'What time is it?'

Rosa consulted her Mickey Mouse watch. 'Four o'clock. The last I heard was, they'd made contact on the telephone but that was all. In the morning we'll go to the consulate.'

'It's nearly dawn. Look.'

'Mmn.' Rosa yawned. 'You know, I've just realised something. I'm not responsible for anyone and no one is for me. No parents, no children, no husband. I see now what they mean by hostages to fortune. So I couldn't be going through the hell you are, or Nick must be. I wonder if I mind. I suppose one day, if I couldn't work, I'd mind very much. The way I live is putting all my eggs in one basket. But then if I couldn't work, I'm not sure I'd want to live, on any terms.'

Rosa rarely spoke so reflectively. Sombre thought was not her way. She peopled the earth with her wonderful giants – visions of Gog and Magog, Titans, kings, queens, colossi – which seemed to say, Look how the human spirit could be! But had no idea what she was doing, Mary guessed, would roar with laughter if you told her. In friendship (and in bed) she was bountiful. Yet in the core of her being she was a nun, vowed to her work.

Mary nodded. The slatted square of black window was now grey. She pushed aside the net and opened the shutters. Looking down on the trees and the chairs tipped two-legged against the tables, listening to the absolute silence of the town, she thought: four o'clock, the dying time.

'I wonder where Joe's got to? Perhaps I could find Hugo Cross?' Then she remembered: 'I don't know where he lives.'

'In a coffin, I should think,' said Rosa. 'Or perhaps he hangs like a bat from a beam at night.'

Mary managed a smile. 'I think he just sort of melts, and the particles come together at dawn. Actually, he's probably with the police, interpreting.' She sank down on the basket chair. She felt as though she had been walking all night. On an impulse, she almost told Rosa about the quarrel with Nick last night, but something fastidious in her, and something ashamed, held her back. This unfinished business was none but hers and Nick's. If I see him alive, if he is returned to me, I shall never be angry with him again, she pledged, like a child making promises to God.

She drowsed and in her half-sleep walked again the city of her dreams, but this time it was different, peopled, throngs pressed around her, running, nearly trampling her, teasing her, pulling her hair, pressing her back when it was most vital to go on. Then there was a dull thud, like a muffled explosion, and she jerked awake to find at the door one of the Pension staff, without his verdigris plumes, simply in trousers and grease-spotted shirt, like a starling stripped of its wings. The thud had been his knocking. Rosa too had slept, still did, she groaned and turned over. Mary, dazed, indicated her sleeping friend, the need for quiet.

'*Qu'est-ce qui se passe?* What is it?' She rubbed her hand across her face.

'Missis. Man attends. Come with me, Missis.'

Nicholas?

'Who is it?' Mary asked, talking too fast for him. 'Is it my husband, is he free? Why doesn't he come up?' Or was it the worst, the worst news she could have? A mad woman, frantic, she pushed past the waiter and ran, nearly tripping, down the stairs. He was standing among the ferns in the lobby of the old ladies, the gossips, the *tricoteuses*. Hugo Cross.

No knitting ladies now. Just the waiter doubling as night porter, yawning over his newspaper.

'You want coffee? Or something stronger?'

Mary shook her head. For once his linen suit was rumpled. He looked weary. They sat in the small dining-room, the room they had been driven to on the night of the storm. Chairs were stacked on tables, but Cross lifted down a couple. At the far end a woman was scrubbing the marble floor – splash, rub, squish. She wore a kerchief knotted at the back of her neck. She used no kneeling pad. Her arms were thick. She advanced towards them, very slowly. The Martini ashtray on their table brimmed with sour butts.

'There are two, we think, three at the most. PLP, PLO, Black September, Red Army, Baader-Meinhof – God knows what they're calling themselves now.'

'But that's broken up, isn't it?' she said (as though it mattered). 'They're both dead, aren't they – Baader and Meinhof?'

A twitch of a smile at the corner of his mouth. 'Their souls go marching on. Anyhow, we've got their terms. They want all political prisoners freed in the Federal Republic of Germany.'

Mary thought, this is how one would receive the news of a terminal disease from a doctor who had seen too much death. Absurdly, one would attempt to hold down hysteria.

'And if not? I mean, if the Germans won't?'

Hugo Cross had ordered coffee for himself and now the night porter shuffled in. They were silent until he had gone, then Cross, stirring his treacly coffee, glanced up, seemed to be measuring her. To see how much I can take, wondered Mary? She sat up straight, her hands locked under the table.

Cross said, 'Then they will shoot the hostages, one by one. That's the usual threat, of course, not necessarily carried through. Just one of the lessons learned in training school.'

'So what's happening? Who's negotiating?'

'The Minister for Sport at the moment – the rest are at some jamboree on the Black Sea by courtesy of the Soviets. They'll come trotting back, of course. Then there is a twitter of consuls. And I must get back and carry on interpreting.' He stood, resting his hand on the back of his chair.

'It was very good of you to tell me.'

'Not at all.'

'How many languages do you speak?'

'Seven,' he said, with that little smile, making leave to go. 'Seven, not counting the dead.'

The scrubbing woman was getting closer, emptying the

ashtrays into one bucket, squeezing her cloth into another. She dragged the two buckets across the marble and now she was at Mary's feet.

'I'm sorry,' said Mary, knowing well enough the woman would not understand, 'I'm in your way.'

The woman looked up and grinned, flashing a gold tooth – the rest were rotten. She might have been thirty-five or sixty-five. Mary suddenly wished she could communicate with her and was reminded of the taxi-driver with his crucifix and carnation. She was seized by a longing for someone, like the woman, like the taxi-driver, to tell her *this* is life, the ordinary sum of things, you will return to it. To the scent of their soap at home, clean white curtains in a breeze, flowers, bills, library tickets, her own waxed floors. A litany in her mind, one she must cling to, repeat, as one tells the beads of a rosary. To know that this ordeal was an aberration, simply a flaw in the peacefully woven texture of her life.

When her mother was dying, Mary remembered, drifting in and out of coma, she woke to speak of things like that: a necklace she had had as a child, bottling fruit, a seaside holiday.

Though she could not understand Mary, the woman sat back on her haunches, her face red with effort, her hands chapped; she arched her back and groaned, still grinning, and spoke in her own language of which Mary caught not the meaning but the message: Mary was not to move, she was sad, she must not be sad – in spite of the harshness of the consonants and the blurred vowels, the laughing speed of her talk, it was like a song, a chant of hope. Then the woman put her roughened hand on Mary's. Just for a moment, that human touch from a stranger meant, oddly, more than the succour of all her friends.

In the lobby – the day now truly begun – Mary was seized in hairy giant paws and squashed against a prickly beard.

'Mary! Maria! My poor sweet soul.'

'Joe, you look awful. Where have you been?'

'Girdling the earth for you, Maria.'

'You want a shower and some coffee. Black. I take it you found nothing helpful?'

He wagged his head sadly, like a large beaten dog who has failed to bring home a bone. Mary was not at all sure she could be bothered with Joe Porterhouse now. She could offer him no response. Their little crowd – their group – among whom it had always been natural to kiss on each cheek, embrace with ritual cries of pleasure, appeared, with the possible exception of Rosa, irrelevant. In any case, most of them were locked up in the Tea Room.

Outside, among the breakfast tables, the other delegates fretted: children with no one to tell them what to do. There was a shamed excitement at this unlooked-for drama and when Mary tried to take her coffee alone, at a corner table, she found herself the object of attention. Everyone had theories. Many approached her as one might a widow, voices hushed. A German woman she had never met before in her life embraced her. A number imagined that she would have some answer because she was the most closely involved in the situation.

'I don't know. I don't know,' she repeated, retreating to the lobby, and as she struggled to explain to the desk-clerk that she wanted to telephone England, to make a connection to England, *Angleterre*, to this number if he would connect her with the exchange or if he would give her the IDD number for England, Britain, the United Kingdom – through all this screeching and head-wagging, hand-wringing and sighing – Mary realised that today would go on like this, and perhaps the next day and the next. Finally, from a great distance, she heard a voice that might have been Chrissie's but Chrissie could not hear her. Mary shouted, gave up, sagged. The desk-clerk was watering the ferns. He had shrugged off this nonsense of telephoning to England. He lived alone in a room he kept very neat and disliked the untidiness of the goings-on that first the Congress, then the hi-jack, had brought upon the Pension. If people would stay in their countries it seemed to him that the world would be saved much strife. Internationalism – he told his canary at home as he shined his narrow black shoes – is the death of peace. Also, he suspected that the night-porter was poisoning his ferns; more than once he had found a cigar butt buried in their pots.

And now this English madwoman was saying she could not get through, or so he understood. Then she was saying more that he could not understand. He sighed and gave her the only advice he could.

'What did he say?' said Rosa, up now and smoking her breakfast all over the ferns. 'Who's Gross? Why have you got to see this Gross?'

'I think he meant Hugo Cross.'

'What does Hugo Cross have to do with telegrams? You asked him how to send a telegram.'

'Perhaps he thought,' said Mary faintly, 'that Hugo Cross could find out what I wanted and interpret.'

'Where the hell is Cross, anyway?'

'He came when you were asleep. I think he's trying to be helpful.'

'He's sneaky. Haven't you noticed? Look down a drain and there's Hugo Cross.'

'Here's Joe.'

On and off, Joe, less ebullient than usual, and Rosa, loyal and grim, escorted Mary through a day of questions and questionings, both wearying, garbled information, false hope, horror, tedium and farce. The sense of farce was strange. More than once Mary remembered her spontaneous reaction when Rosa, weeping, first ran to her from the Tea Room: her laughter. But this was absurd. It must be a joke.

Everywhere there were rumours: that the hostages had been shot, that they were about to be freed in exchange for a sum of money and a flight to a destination of their choice for the terrorists. That the Minister of Sport had himself spoken to the terrorists. That there had been a blackout of news coverage. (This was true enough – one of the militia, who had taken over from the police on the quarantined promenade, smashed an Italian journalist's camera with his rifle butt.)

Out of the babble downstairs, Mary was shown into the room of the chief of police. He looked tired, as though he had not slept, and there was a button missing from his cuff. Absurd that one should notice such things at a time like this. Joe had disappeared again (he doesn't like the fuzz, Rosa hissed), so the two women were alone with the tired man, who spoke no English or said, in fractured French, that he spoke no English, but there would be coming a person. He had dirty fingernails, every so often shouted into the telephone, and chain-smoked yellow cigarettes. Mary supposed the person would be an interpreter – presumably Hugo Cross – closed her eyes momentarily and opened them to see Count Dobi bending over her.

'My poor Missis Lamb,' he murmured. 'I am your interpreter. If I could do more –' The scent she remembered, of sandalwood, and some oil; his touch as he took her hand was slightly damp but cool.

She drew back. 'If we could get this interview done as soon as possible?' There was something almost womanish about him – not gay, but like a man in drag. An hermaphrodite?

And then, it appeared, she was to get not answers but questions.

What was the last time she saw her husband? Why was she not at the meeting in the Tea Room herself? Why was Miss Treadwell not at the meeting? The policeman snapped the questions and Dobi delivered them with a stroking regret, like a host apologising for the manners of his servants. What were the political affiliations of the hostages in the Tea Room? How many were Jewish? What was the subject of the meeting the day of the hi-jack?

'For God's sake,' yelled Rosa, 'd'you think they kidnapped themselves?'

'I'm sorry,' said Mary quietly. 'I am answering no more questions except in the presence of the British consul. All I am concerned with is the safety of my husband and his colleagues.'

Outside, Joe was waiting for them in a cab. Rosa collapsed, gasping with rage. 'That ridiculous man with the slimy eyes. He looked like a pimp.'

Mary followed and sat down beside her. 'Dobi?' she said. 'He is.'

Then there was Piper, of the British consulate: a desiccated stick-insect who offered tea and a spoonful of sympathy but not much else. Bailing out stranded tourists was more his line, ha ha. Retiring soon and due to go on leave when this thing blew up. Advice from home was a low profile. He tidied papers on his desk, already tidy, and in the same tone of an embarrassed housemaster delivering bad news of a personal nature, took off his spectacles and said to the air, 'Your colleagues, you know, the Congress. One really does feel they should pack their bags. Difficult times. Inflammatory situation. Though strictly one's concern is only for British nationals.'

Even quietly frantic as she was, hysteria held down, Mary saw Piper, his skin drying to the colour of sand, his hair greying through a lifetime of offices like this – little English jokes far from home – now at his last posting cruelly awakened from his doze by an outrage beyond his experience. Yet why should it be beyond his experience, his ability to cope? Such things were happening every day, all over the world, and here they were, in this office, talking as though the terrible situation involving her husband and her friends were hypothetical. That awful English retreat from bother or pain. Suddenly, Mary was not merely distraught but angry.

'I want to know what is being done. What is the reaction from Germany? Who is officially negotiating? What line is the Foreign Office taking, and why haven't they sent someone from England?'

'Ah, well, yes.' Piper pulled his nose and glanced at the telephone, the door, as though for rescue. 'This is unusual, you see, there is no precedent one is aware of for this kind of terrorist gesture in a left-wing country. Teheran, of course, but that was in a revolutionary context with a fanatical government. We're on pretty good terms with the chappies here. And there are only three terrorists to deal with. The Committee should be able to bag them easily enough. But I must emphasise, Mrs er-Lamb, that with so many governments involved one can't have them all around pressing their claims. What a garden-party that would be! So the fewer foreign nationals, altogether, the better.'

'Did you say *three* terrorists?'

'Yes. It appears that there had been an inside man, a waiter.'

Piper looked at the telephone. It rang. He seized it with relief, said yes, no, listened. Mary stood to leave. Piper put his hand over the receiver.

'I say. I am terribly sorry, you know.'

Mary nodded. Perhaps he really was.

Back at the Pension, there had been some kind of drama. Luggage was heaped under the trees. Passengers were climbing into the airport coach. Mary recognised the German woman who had embraced her that morning, struggling to heave on to the bus every one of her parcels and boxes and straw hats and baskets, like a fat child who won't leave her toys behind. Jostling her in a most ungentlemanly way was Waldemar's appalling American-speaking Swede.

'Blessed be the Lord,' grinned Joe, as Mary and Rosa stepped from the taxi. 'Thought I'd have to drink alone.'

'What's going on?'

'Notice to quit. End of teddybears' picnic.'

'You mean the Congress?' Mary sank down and accepted the drink Joe pushed towards her. It didn't matter what it was. 'Well, obviously that couldn't go on.'

'No – trippers too. They've been advised by the Minister of Tourism.'

'Because of the Tea Room business? Or is there something else?'

Joe shrugged, squeezed Rosa's bare thigh under the table. She kicked him. Was Joe Porterhouse really the clown he made out, Mary wondered? The big-handed fat man, the burned-out journalist you met in every bar from Marseilles south? In films, at least. She forced herself to swallow her drink like medicine. I'm being silly, she thought, seeing bears on the stairs.

'Have you heard anything? Have you seen Hugo Cross?'

'Not in my *estaminet*.'

'Then that must be good? Nothing's happened?' One day won for Nick. How many more? Whatever Piper said, it could be like Teheran. How did one live like that? For months, for years? I have been spoiled, she thought, watching the airport coach draw away. I have led a charmed life.

'I've just remembered,' said Rosa. 'Something about that girl, the blonde, I noticed before I started to run. She was wearing a gold chain round her ankle.'

Mary frowned. Then she recalled the fair girl and the boy that day in the café – could it have been? In this country, she mused, this land of my dreams, now of nightmare, anything is possible – or, rather, nothing is impossible. Reason and sense are garbled: in the Byzantine church, in the hill village, one speaks and nonsense is returned. *Having found her way past the guardians into the secret place, Deborah spoke out clearly and politely, as she had been taught, but all the people would ever do was to repeat what she had said, though never exactly as she had said it.*

Mary must have fallen asleep, fully dressed, on her bed. She awoke to the sound of shouts, gunfire and running feet.

7

Nancy Prewitt squealed: 'What was that?'

Gwendell was immediately awake. She had this gift – like some birds, she claimed – of sleeping with only half her brain: useful in emergencies, of which she had known many. 'The United States Cavalry, I imagine? To the rescue?'

Nicholas shook his head. 'Too far away. It must have come from the middle of town.' He was impressed by the way that Nancy, after her first panic, had collected herself – a courage that meant so much more than Gwendell's natural lack of fear. It was easy to make jokes about Nancy Prewitt, and unfair. Firmly, he took her hand and whispered, 'Well, this is one place the French can't walk out of.' The firing bothered him though. Mary – he had hardly allowed himself to think of her since all this started. Alone, he could cope, he imagined, though he credited himself with no special bravery; but if Mary were in danger too, that could undo him.

The shots had startled their captors and brought the third from the kitchen – still dressed absurdly in a waiter's white jacket. They held some kind of quick, whispered parley, then the kitchen telephone rang. The girl went to answer it, came back, and after consultation with the other two, barked at the hostages, 'You will stand, one by one, to have your hands bound in front of you.' This second night, after the long period sitting against the wall, little exercise by day, their limbs were cramped and Waldemar, in particular, had difficulty in standing. They sat again, the wire chafed their wrists. Nicholas noticed when it came to his turn, that the dark boy's own hands were trembling. Finally – rather in the manner of an ungracious air hostess addressing nervous passengers in a thunderstorm – the girl, Helga, announced, 'The shooting you have just heard has nothing to do with you. You are not to be rescued.'

'Might one ask what it was?' In the shuttered room, in the single dim light the terrorists permitted, Waldemar looked fragile, like old paper, as though a puff might crumble him.

'A civil disturbance,' she conceded. 'No more questions.'

That little excitement over, even those who had managed to doze before could sleep no more. Perhaps the girl had told the truth, Nicholas wondered – they'd gathered from Hugo Cross that the Committee had an uncertain hold on the country, and factions within. Then, ever since the death of the Old Man the world had been waiting for the Soviets to make their grab. Nicholas wished he had been less idle politically. Competence in committee, a modest gift for teaching and a slim volume on the metaphysical poets, did not, alas, equip one for survival. Nancy was talking.

'I remember when I was small, in the war, going to a zoo. I didn't like the animals being behind bars – especially the big apes, they looked so human, so sad – then the warning went. It was quite a bad raid. I thought, how awful to be a prisoner like that, with a war going on outside. You'd have thought they'd have evacuated them, wouldn't you?'

Nicholas nodded. 'I don't think it's a war out there, though. Probably just what the girl said. And our keepers are inside the cage with us.'

Nancy gave the small gasp she always did when she realised she had said the wrong thing. Or when she imagined that to be the case, which was often.

'Oh, I'm sorry! I didn't think! You must be dreadfully worried about Mary. She is so lovely. Everyone loves Mary.'

Poor Prewitt, thought Nicholas. We must get out of the habit of calling her poor Prewitt. Do people live down as well as up to other's expectations of them? Like children catching the tone of their parents' bedtime talk in another room? If one were to say happy and beautiful Nancy, would Poor Prewitt dissolve, exorcised, into thin air? Mary and I – we love our friends. Should we try harder to love Prewitt?

And what an odd speculation in the circumstances – unless at the back of his mind were the tactics he and Waldemar had tried to use on the terrorists. Talk to them quietly, whenever possible individually, smile, draw them out, get them to talk about themselves. The prescribed treatment. One had read the books and the newspaper reports. Proven theory: it is difficult for even these dangerous children to kill someone they know well. Surprising attachments have been formed between captors and prisoners, a symbiotic interdependence. Or so it was once, in what looked now like the innocent days of terrorism: the Spaghetti House siege, that Dutchman in Ireland. Nicholas and Waldemar had discussed all this in whispers last night, deploring Manzarotti's clumsy attack. Neither had mentioned Iran. Those almost forgotten prisoners scattered God or Allah knew where, in the middle of a war. Poor Nancy's helpless apes.

So yesterday Waldemar had taken on the girl again. At first she had resisted, then, just perceptibly, weakened before the Swede's charm. He had taken care to ask no questions or favours, simply talked, in his mild, hypnotic sing-song, as though all – captors and prisoners – were railway passengers inconvenienced by some delay. Nicholas, meanwhile had offered English cigarettes to the Arab boy, Ali, rather shy. He was sensitive, a student he said (wasn't everyone nowadays?), edgy when Helga was in earshot, almost pathetically anxious to establish good relations when she was not.

And Gwendell – oh, Gwendell was Gwendell, that is to say,

marvellous! Within five minutes of his appearance from the kitchen, sometime round noon, she had Hernandes – a round-faced cheerful boy, Portuguese, a bit of a clown – fetching and carrying for her. Olives, bread, some dry ham, cakes, mineral water for Waldemar. A cushion for her back. The story of his life. 'Oh, but how interesting,' she boomed, 'how kind. How very amusing. What a dear boy.'

Yet these are games, Nicholas thought now, through the nightwatch, ploys, desperate games. Nancy slept at last and her head dropped on to his shoulder. (How shocked she would be when she woke!) On the other side, Waldemar, he could tell, did not sleep. Nicholas whispered.

'What's the price, d'you think?'

'My guess is it's the gang who took a pot-shot at the Swedish ambassador in Bonn. Quite small stuff, really,' he sighed, 'but unfortunate for us. Schmidt's statement as far back as Mogadishu made it quite clear there would be no deals. Absolutely correct, of course.' He shifted his position and winced. That little smile, like a glimpse of pale sun on snow: 'It is interesting how different things look from the other side of the fence. I have supported the hard line myself, with regret. Even so, it goes on, and escalates: a pandemic. It is almost pure violence now – the cause of little importance, the perpetrator and victim even less.'

Nicholas almost smiled. Terrible and dramatic though their circumstances were – Waldemar himself most personally afflicted – still, in the eyes of the gentle Swede (who had been known to stop a meeting to let a butterfly out of the window) there was that glint of academic passion. Every act or circumstance to be viewed from all angles and filtered through the intellect. Years ago, on a Connecticut beach, Nicholas – enjoying a Fulbright at Harvard – had been among others watching from the beach while Waldemar, all arms and legs, perilously negotiated a sailing dinghy. A huff of wind and three or four of the pretty boats capsized. All were righted except Waldemar's. No one worried too much until their hostess screamed, 'My God! He can't swim!'

Rescued and laid out on the beach to dry, their visiting Professor in Old Icelandic finally opened his eyes and explained,

'It's not true, you know. Your life does not pass before you.'

'But Waldy, why didn't you shout? What were you *doing*?'

'Drowning?'

Remembering, with amusement and fondness this little incident – a scene from another world of ordinariness and laughter – Nicholas had not caught Waldemar's last murmured remark.

'I'm sorry?'

Waldemar nodded without expression, as at a pupil who had dozed off in a tutorial.

'This Fascist thing will not be so funny quite soon, I think, and then the time will come again for the Jews.'

'Oh, surely not! Since Israel. That could never happen again.'

In the sickly light, his long neck stretched, the back of his head resting – so far as one could rest – against the wall, the Swede aged from the Monsieur Hulot of international committees to a tired prophet. Of course, he was old, quite old, and not well.

'Not the new Jews, not Israel. History is a lighthouse, you see. It has a far-reaching loom, but sometimes one must look closer to home. The little shopkeeper in Paris, the rabbi, the European Jews – they are still vulnerable. The first synagogue that is bombed, we shall see.' He raised both manacled hands to his face as if to wipe away some dusty thought. 'The lighthouse!' he said, with disgust. 'You know that not once has the General Assembly passed a resolution to outlaw terrorism! Oh, the Hague Convention, yes. But that was ten years ago. And how many of the Third World countries have signed? I used to believe, you know, but now I think: that Tower of Babel and folly, that Disunited Nations, that lighthouse of blind men!'

Gwendell awoke with a snort. 'Nicholas – you are exciting Waldemar and he is not to be excited. I forbid it.'

The Swede patted her hand, as well as he could with his wired wrists. 'My dear, I am quite well.'

'You are not well and you are shouting. Tomorrow I shall get that nice little Hernandes to send for your tummy medicine. And my knitting.'

Nicholas grinned. 'Darling Gwendell, this is not a hotel and outside they appear to be shooting each other.'

'Stuff and nonsense, the whole thing.'

'Tell that to our hosts.'

'Oh, I have, I have. Miss Helga was quite rude, but I believe Hernandes understood. Myself, I have never grasped why people need to hurt each other. It appals me more, almost, than cruelty to animals.' That was true, as many a mule-owner or camel-driver had discovered to his cost and astonishment – upbraided by this large, strange, white, foreign female, swooping upon them like a dust demon, while they mildly kicked their beasts. 'Poor Manzarotti, you know, I have little time for the man, but he is hurt quite badly.'

'In his head?'

'In his Marxism. One can see.'

Nicholas yawned. He felt penitent to have thought so little of Mary, but it was extraordinary what concentration such an ordeal required. As if he had been born, brought up and now might die in this room. He tried to think himself to sleep with words, with poetry, with Herbert, his favourite. *The harbingers are come. See, see their mark; white is their colour, and behold my head. But must they have my brain? must they dispark those sparkling notions, which therein were bred?* But no God here, dear George, no saving grace.

Dawn. In a shallow doze he had chafed his wrists and there was blood. The girl nosed open a slat of the shutters with her rifle and a bleak grey sea-light trickled through, lay in a dull pool at their feet.

Another day.

8

'But I have the code. It *must* be right!' Mary sweated at the lobby telephone. She covered the mouthpiece with her hand and turned to Rosa, who was gassing the ferns with her Gauloises.

'All I get is this damned recording, first in the local gobbledygook, then in French, telling me that the number is discontinued, please to consult my documentation of something. Then I get this so-called international operator, who routes me through Paris where Peter Sellers or the Pink Panther tells me England is out of order. And now I'm cut off – the phone's dead.'

'Well it is out of order.'

'What?'

'England.'

Miraculously, in the circumstances, coffee did appear.

'And then,' said Rosa, 'there was last night's bloody revolution. Or whatever it was. It seems quiet enough now. And you musn't worry about Chrissie – she'll have her baby with or without you. And talking to her won't help Nick.'

Mary nodded absently. Finally she said, 'There are no papers, you know, nothing; just the radio – someone yelling something. And look – there's no one in the streets.' Her dream, she thought – the empty city. 'I must find Hugo Cross. Where's Joe?'

'Sloped off, the slob, when the firing started. Crept back at dawn and snoring his head off now. He says it's some left-wing coup and we're all to get out. They're closing the airport.'

'I'm not going without Nick.'

Rosa sighed and nodded. Now the mist had lifted from the sea it was a morning of cruel perfection: the air trembled with advancing gold. But the waiter who had served them coffee hung over them, fidgeted, fussed with his tray, clicked and hissed until Mary finally came out of her dream.

'Yes?'

He looked nervous; no longer the figure of shabby authority who waged war on carnation sellers.

'Missis,' he hissed urgently, '*dames*. Go. *Allez!* Away!' He flapped his white cloth as he had at the carnation man.

'Why? Where are we to go? *Où? Dove?*'

'Go away! Bad, not stay. Bang, bang!'

'Yes,' said Rosa. 'We heard the bang, bang too.'

'Thank you,' said Mary and felt vaguely that they should tip him. His intentions were good. But he was gone, wagging his head, clicking to himself, presumably, about the idiocy of foreign females who refused to fly away.

Not that they had refused. Not that they had agreed. They sat unspeaking. The familiar black limousine slid along the promenade, then the view was empty again. Rosa ground out her cigarette and pushed back her chair.

'I'm going in to kick Porterhouse.'

Mary nodded. She sat on, put a coin under her coffee cup, and made up her mind.

Light-headed from lack of sleep and the shock in the night, Mary knew, even before she turned the corner on the promenade, that the armoured vans would have gone from around the English Tea Room. The shutters were still closed but only a solitary guard – a soldier, she imagined – lounged outside. To keep intruders out or escapers in? She had no idea, but stepped back into the shadow and walked quickly away. Twice she was frustrated in the winding, narrow streets, coming upon the same square with a dry fountain in the centre. Once, she ducked into a doorway as a small, grey-painted armoured vehicle swayed past – no more than a jeep with a gun really. It must have been nine o'clock now. Normally the city would have been bustling hours ago with those who set the stage for the day to begin, but today from behind closed doors and shuttered windows, there was a tangible listening. It was startling to see a child run out laughing into the street; a woman snatched her back in, slapping and kissing. Just for a second, Mary glimpsed the interior that had swallowed the mother and child – a man at a table in shirtsleeves, a beaded curtain, a canary in a cage – and had a crazy impulse to run in, seek sanctuary. Just as she turned at last into the more modern architecture of the street that housed the consulate a voice shouted after her. She found the modest brass notice let into the wall like a dentist's plate and pressed the bell.

'Well, that, you see, is it,' said Peter Piper, the stick-man. This morning he looked as though he had not just picked but eaten a peck of pickled pepper. 'Closing shop.'

Mary sagged in the chair on the other side of the desk behind which Piper opened and closed drawers, counted keys, rose twice to thrust his beak into filing cabinets, withdraw papers and lock.

'You mean you're leaving? Closing the consulate?'

'Well, not exactly.' He did, at last, sit still. 'Lying doggo more. A token presence, if you see what I mean.'

'No, I don't.' The thought flicked across Mary's mind: how I have changed. She who set out to please and did so effortlessly, rarely rebuffed, now shouts at telephonists and bullies consuls.

Piper seemed to visit briefly some other sphere and then return to her.

'Well, you wouldn't, you see, you don't know the ropes. How could you?'

'Perhaps you could tell me the ropes.'

'Ah yes, well now. It seemed, you see, in view of that fuss in the night, rather a good idea for the ambassador to remember a small but pressing appointment in a high place in Italy. Likewise the consul and proconsul. Just until we know where we are. Not a recall, you understand, not at all. But if, by chance, the Soviets were involved – which remains to be seen – the embarrassment would be lessened all round. That is, since he is not here, he could not officially be recalled. Nor would he be obliged to consort. Naturally, if it were decided elsewhere that a hard line might be desirable, he would then return so that he might be recalled. If you follow me.'

'Is this how politics work?'

'Usually.'

'Then what are you doing here? I thought you were the consul?'

'Vice-consul. As I said, a presence. Awaiting the turn of events and further instructions. Anything I can do, of course. I'd offer you tea but the girl's done a bunk and the cupboard is locked. Brandy perhaps? A little *fine*?'

At first, Mary felt no; then, bemused, nodded, and swallowed a glass of the brandy Piper produced from a deep drawer. She had felt insubstantial before. Now she was floating and heard Piper's voice from a great distance. He seemed more relaxed, less brittle of limb, almost cosy.

'Had leave coming up, you know, then really I was out to grass.'

'Where were you retiring to? You have a family?' It seemed unlikely.

'Once,' he said. 'A wife.' For a second his expression was ragged with grief and memory, then bland again. No one, thought Mary, is entirely a joke. It might have been the brandy but she felt an impulse to be nicer to Piper. 'No.' he went on, 'dropping anchor at a little guesthouse in the Lakes. Grasmere – that's funny, isn't it: put out to grass.' He refilled their glasses. 'I'll tell you something, you know – I do miss the rain. The skies at home: always changing. That light.' He put down his glass and she could imagine him later, rinsing and drying it carefully. 'Ah well,' he concluded, 'mustn't keep you. You'll be off to the airport.'

And what did Alice do then? thought Mary.

'I'm going nowhere while my husband is still a hostage.'

'Oh dear. Of course.' For the first time Piper appeared truly to focus on Mary. 'But, you know, really, I must advise you to leave. Things are most terribly unstable and there is nothing you can do, not at all. As I said, we maintain a presence. I'd say you pop off home and all we can do for your husband – for all those unfortunates indeed – we shall do.'

He's talking, Mary thought, as if Nick were dead. What will he promise next? A decent burial? The alcohol on an empty stomach was having its depressive after-effect. Could it go on like this, until, in six months, in a year, the hostages were forgotten? While she would wander for ever in this world through the looking-glass. She picked up her shoulder-bag and remembered why she had come.

'There's one thing you can do for me. Can you give me Hugo Cross's address?'

Piper seemed startled. 'Cross?'

'The Council man.'

'Ah yes. Cross. Funny chap.' Piper stood, unlocked one of the many cabinets he had locked, took out a card. 'Somewhere in the market, I believe – rum place to live.' He was copying from the card on to a piece of paper, which he folded and handed over with reluctance, she felt. 'I do hope you're not planning an excursion alone? Especially in the present circumstances?'

Mary smiled. She felt better with the paper in her hand. Without reason. 'He warned me off, too. How funny.'

Piper looked so worried, she liked him again. She turned at the door. 'Thank you for the drink. I hope you get to Grasmere.'

He accompanied her to the heavy outer door, opened it for her and watched her down the street. He should not, he felt, have let her go – but what else he might have done, he had no idea.

The explosion came at mid-morning, just as they were allowed, in turn, to take their exercise around the room. Even inside, with the windows shuttered, they had sensed the following silence, felt it palpably – a frisson just beneath the skin. As though a beast crouched outside, holding its breath. Then the telephone was cut off and their captors seemed as tense, as listening, as the hostages. When the silence was broken again, as shocked. For a moment the glances they exchanged, terrorists and victims, might have been those of companions sharing the same danger. The Frenchman, Fourges, whose turn it had been to walk, sat down again. There was a crackle of firing, like rain on a tin roof, running feet, shouts and the thunderous rumbling of some heavy vehicle.

No one spoke. Nicholas was reminded of childhood, air-raid shelters in the war: the hush as one waited for the hit, the shaky jokes afterwards.

Waldemar let out a little breath, a disguised groan. He was bent double.

Gwendell spoke first, sharply. 'Someone get that damned wire off his wrists. He's sick. Can't you see?'

The boy, Ali, glanced at Helga and she nodded. He knelt before Waldemar's slumped figure and freed the old man's wrists, very gently. He might have been tending his own father.

Mary could not tell from where the explosion came. She felt at the epicentre – it seemed all around her, echoing from the taller buildings, shaking the narrow side-alleys. Someone was firing, then a man, crouched, ran across the street and threw a grenade. Mary covered her ears and ducked against the wall, then ran.

At the entrance to the market a crowd of men and boys pressed against her, shouting, some bearing flags, rifles, placards waving above their heads, and in the shouting she detected a chant she could not understand: a name, a cry, an ululation that made of the advancing mass one roaring creature, agape, triumphant, hungry. Market stalls were toppled – yesterday's wilted flowers and perished fruit trampled underfoot – and, attempting not to be forced back when she wished to go forward, Mary herself was knocked to her knees. She clung to something iron, a wrought-iron gate, ducked her head and shielded her face with her arm. They meant her no harm, she sensed, they did not see her – even the man whose boot thudded against her jaw – but on and on they came, chanting, chanting. There was the crack of a rifle (a sniper?) and a boy fell heavily against her. The firing was returned, the boy dragged away by his comrades, and the square was empty. In the silence a dusty pigeon inspected the ruins.

Mary was almost fainting against the grille in the heavy door. The woman, grumbling and suspicious, finally let her in, preceded her up the stone stairs, and from a heavy bunch of keys took one and turned it in the lock.

Once, she woke from her faint or her sleep and looked round. Cross's room was like a monk's cell. The hard bed-divan on which she lay, the plain table that served, she guessed hazily, for meals and work. White-painted walls, a couple of chairs, a cupboard. Window. No curtain. Something brighter – rich? She slept again.

The dream came. The same streets, buildings, a city unpeopled as though by a neutron bomb. But this time she was running, gasping, searching for something, someone, lost; on the leaden legs of dream she ran, would always be running, never arrive. She was not alone. A man stood with his back to her, watching the sea. She called. He would not turn. She called. She heard someone screaming. Herself.

'You were dreaming.'

Hugo Cross stood over her. A finger of sun blinded Mary, making Cross's face opaque; a man without features. She put up her arm to shield her eyes from the light and gasped with pain.

'I'm sorry,' she said. 'There's blood on your cushion.' She remembered now, hazily, the blow to the jaw; but so much blood? It hurt to speak. 'If you've got water? A cloth? The bathroom?'

'Stay there. You've been hurt. I'll fetch them.'

While he was out of the room, Mary groped painfully for her bag and, in it, the compact mirror. Sweat had coiled her naturally curly hair into Medusa snakes, her jaw was swollen, cut and bruised, and the whole side of her face, her dress, even her arm, were caked with blood. She lowered her feet to the floor, paused to test her balance, and awkwardly stood, then, grasping the door-frame, then the wall, walked in the direction Cross had gone. There was a passage and a bathroom. Cross was filling a bowl with water.

'No. Really, I can do it.' It was painful to smile. 'Such a mess.'

But after all, she did feel dizzy; so, absurdly somehow, she sat like a child on a wooden stool while Cross sponged her face. She closed her eyes against the stinging soap. For one normally so dextrous, he was gentle but clumsy, and Mary remembered thinking, he doesn't like to be touched. Or to touch, she guessed: I've embarrassed him. 'That's lovely,' she said, 'I can do my arm myself,' and opened her eyes. He was still bent over her. For a second his face was very close to hers, his pale eyes studying her, the flicker of a question, of wonder? Then he turned away, squeezed out the sponge and handed it to her. 'If you're sure?'

'Yes.'

'Then I'll make some coffee.'

'Lovely.' She thought: why do I keep saying lovely?

'Shout if you want anything.'

'Yes. Thank you.' She looked down at her dress: just the one arm torn but still so much blood. 'If I could rinse this through it would be dry enough in an hour?'

He nodded. 'I'll get you something.'

It was a kaftan, cotton, very cool, loosely cut; the pattern, a most delicate fingering of pale leaves and birds. She lingered in the bathroom: shaver, toothbrush, sponge, glass, aspirin on a shelf, comb, towel – minimal signs of human habitation. No clues here. Clues to what? The blood had not dried and washed out easily. She hung her dress from a hook in the tiled shower and watched the rusty water run away, reminding her of something. Menstruation. Child-birth. Chrissie falling off her bicycle when she was seven, eight; only a little cut but there was so much blood.

'This kaftan is beautiful,' she said. 'Whose is it?'

'Mine.' Cross looked up from the table. He seemed easier now. Though still on guard he had, while Mary was in the bathroom, retaken possession of his own territory, so surprisingly invaded. 'They're a symbol of immortality, you know. The birds.' He set down the coffee cups with the ceremony and precision – exactly so – of a geisha.

'*Café filtre*,' Mary said. 'What a treat. A change from Turkish treacle.' They waited for the coffee to drip through the paper. 'D'you hope to live for ever then?'

'I hope not.'

She sank back against the small cushions. They drank their coffee.

'It was the boy's blood, too. That's why there was so much blood.' Of course, how silly, he wouldn't know. She still felt hazy. Her head ached badly. Leaving her the divan, Cross sat on a hard chair, with his back to the window. Mary explained. 'There was a boy in the crowd. He was shot and fell against me. He was bleeding terribly. I remember now – they were shouting something.' She put her hand to her throbbing temple. It seemed important to remember. 'I couldn't make it out – it sounded like draha, something like that.'

He nodded. 'Draza. Draza Pleiscu. He's on the left of the Committee – Blok's opponent; but he's weak – not much more than a puppet really. Moscow pulls the strings.'

Mary tried to think clearly. 'So that's what last night's coup or whatever it was, was all about? What happens next? The Russians move in, like Afghanistan?'

'I doubt it. Not yet, anyway. Easier, cheaper and less provocative to let them do it for themselves. But I'm not sure Pleiscu's up to it. Blok's tough.'

'Oh yes. Yes, I'd heard about him. Perhaps you told me.' Mary was finding it increasingly difficult to concentrate. She reached in her bag for her cigarettes and brought out a crumpled packet. Cross stood to light it for her and from nowhere – the air, a cupboard, his pocket? – produced an ashtray. For the first time, Mary was amused. Funny Cross with his monkish ways and beautiful kaftan, little smiles and ashtrays. Mystery hiding nothing, she wondered – or secrets?

'And where do you stand in this?' Why did she always think of him as Cross, never Hugo? Hugo, she thought, weighing it.

'I watch.'

'Part of the wallpaper?'

'Something like that.' He sat on his hard chair again, arms crossed. 'And what were you doing in the market anyway?'

'Looking for you.' Mary stubbed out her cigarette. It made her feel sick. 'Well, I was worried – frantic, of course. And no one seemed to know what was happening, or no one would tell me. Everyone going, the airport closing – the relatives of the hostages can't get in, you know. The phone was cut. I had this terrible feeling that the hostages might just be forgotten. I'd had enough of the police, and anyway, if it was a revolution, I didn't know which side they were on. I just thought you might be able to help, you might know something.'

'I could give you a very good lecture on Forster. In Serbo-Croat.'

'I thought we were supposed to have gone off Forster?'

'I haven't. Have you?'

This is crazy, she thought: Nick might be dead and we're talking about Forster. God help the English.

'So you've no news? No advice?'

'Only to leave. But Peter the Piper will have told you that already.'

'How do you know I've seen Piper?'

He smiled. 'Everyone does at some point. Is he still going home to Grasmere?'

'Still?'

'He's been saying that for years, but he's never seen the Lakes and there's no little guesthouse. He hasn't been home since I've known him.'

'Home?'

'England. His wife died, I believe, and he never went back – nothing to go back for. So when they kick him out he'll die here or somewhere like it.'

'That's rather sad.'

'There's a lot of us about, though not as many as there used to be.'

'No – I mean it's sad that he has to make up a story.'

'Oh, he believes it. It's not made up – his idea of England.'

'And you?'

'Much the same, but no fantasies.'

Mary nodded, had the odd feeling she had known before with Cross, that beneath their conversation there was some other, subterranean dialogue. The sun had left the room now. It must be early evening. 'I should go now, if I can. My dress will be dry.'

'Not a good idea. There are too many people taking pot-shots, I'm afraid. You must stay here.'

'But where?'

'You can have the divan. There's another small room down the corridor.'

'I'm terribly sorry; what a nuisance for you.'

He shook his head. 'I've got to pop out. You rest and we'll have some supper.'

'But you said it was too dangerous?'

'I shall put on my cloak of invisibility. Lock the door behind me.'

When he had gone, Mary stood for a moment and said to the closed door; 'I don't know what to make of you, Mr Hugo Cross.'

Waldemar's collapse had subtly altered the atmosphere in the Tea Room. Hostages and terrorists already had in common that the world appeared to have forgotten them. Now the condition of Waldemar bound them in concern, at least. They were like the representatives of warring nations shipwrecked and adrift on the same raft. Even Helga seemed alarmed, pacing the small room and stopping to stand, frowning, over the old man, as he sat, propped and gasping, his arms crossed and gripping his diaphragm.

'I am sorry,' she said, 'we cannot get medicine. The phone is gone. I have aspirin?'

Then Nancy Prewitt astonished them. 'No,' she said, 'milk. Is there any milk?'

'A little in the kitchen.' Ali scuttled to fetch it.

Nancy said, 'Will you please free my wrists? And lay out those cushions to make a bed.'

The makeshift bed was arranged and, supervised by Nancy, Waldemar helped to it. Nancy got him to lie flat, propped two cushions behind his head and fed him a little of the milk. She crouched by the bed, talking to him quietly until at last his long frame seemed less racked; he lay back and closed his eyes.

Nicholas was impressed. 'However did you know that?'

She smiled, blushed, looked almost pretty. She did look pretty.

'Just a bit of first-aid. At evening classes. I did campanology too. I had a hero who was a bell-ringer. In Hampstead. I mean, I did the classes in Hampstead.'

'That was extremely enterprising.'

'Well, I don't go out very much, you see.' She spoke softly, shy again, dismissing herself. 'And my flat's not really big enough to entertain. To tell you the truth, I'm not very good with people.' She raised her head and smiled. 'I don't have any charm. It seemed to have got left out somehow. I always envy Mary that. Among other things.'

Other things, pondered Nicholas, and found himself surprisingly pleased.

'You think too little of yourself.' And she did look attractive now, still flushed from her small triumph with Waldemar. She was tired, of course, as they all were, from their ordeal, yet her skin had lost its sallow tinge. Her eyes were bright and she smiled as she spoke.

'You know, I nearly didn't come. I never liked this sort of thing. Then such a long way, abroad. At first all I thought about was getting home: I even crossed out the days in my diary, like waiting for the end of term. Though with me, it was always the other way round. I didn't mind school so much, because it was work I wanted to do and we all wore the same uniform. That made me feel safe. At home I always felt they were expecting me to be someone I wasn't: beautiful and clever, like my mother. I mean clever talking, not clever writing – it's quite different. She was a great doer of things, nothing scared her.

'I'm sorry, I'm talking too much. I don't usually talk like this. But this trip – the funny thing is, if they chop off our heads tomorrow, I'm still glad I came. D'you think they will chop off our heads?'

'I don't know,' he answered, truthfully. 'That's what they're taught at the Camp Khayat – the terrorists' finishing school. But even they couldn't have predicted these circumstances. It could go either way.'

'It's odd, isn't it? Just for that moment when Waldemar collapsed, I felt we were all on the same side. Oh Lord, I need that bucket again. This would be a funny place to die. Those extraordinary screens and trellis work, the tables set for two. So elegant!' Someone had come up with a sleeping pill for Waldemar; Nancy settled him by the light of a candle – the power had gone along with the telephone, but there was still water.

'That gel,' said Gwendell, while Nancy had gone behind the screen to use the bucket. 'Not such a fool.' The Dame, thought Nicholas, looked older, tired, less indomitable, as she took her place by Waldemar's head. Hernandes had brought from the kitchen the last absurd éclair, but no one had the stomach for it. Nancy had removed Waldemar's false teeth and he slept raspingly, mouth open. Now she slept, her head against Nicholas's shoulder. *Therefore we can go die as sleep*, pondered Nicholas, but Herbert and his unflagging fight with God and yearning for him, was no help tonight. Words, words, a life of them spoken and written; all those little bone castles of our heads that, even without God, could teem with visions – so easily crumbled. Tomorrow perhaps? Waldemar tonight? It is beginning to smell in here. We no longer regard the sniper fire outside, only sporadic now. Hernandes sleeps like a dog at Waldemar's feet, Ali rubs his eyes. Helga droops over her gun. The light of the single candle makes ghosts of us all.

Mary sat with Cross at the candle-lit table over a supper of salami, bread, salad, fruit and wine.

'Coffee?' he asked. 'I could do it on the primus.'

She shook her head. 'That icon. That's what I saw when I woke before you came – the sun was on it. I just had the impression of something glowing. It's beautiful.' She reached for her glass again. 'No news, I suppose?'

'Pleiscu's gang still have the police station and the telephone exchange. So there's nothing on the hostages, I'm afraid. If the power comes back I'll fiddle with the radio in a minute and try for BBC Overseas. There may be things happening in high places we know nothing about.'

'I don't believe there is very much you don't know. So the left extremists will do *nothing* about the hostages? Even less than before? That's terrible.'

'For them, the hostages are politically irrelevant. A bit of a nuisance, that's all, if the SAS come stamping up the beach.'

'You think that's likely?'

'No.'

They came in partway through, the broadcast as crackling and faint as though it really had crossed seas, climbed mountains: "... relatives of hostages unable to enter country. Deep concern is expressed by the German Chancellor but at a press conference in Bonn tonight he repeated that in no circumstances would the Federal Government surrender to blackmail. The situation has grown increasingly confused in view of the attempted coup, believed to have been instigated by the left-wing followers of Draza Pleiscu, former member of the Committee that has governed the country since the death of the late

President. The whereabouts of Alexis Blok, supporter of the former President's autonomous if autocratic form of government, are unknown. At home, the number of unemployed has risen above the two million mark. In Northern Ireland yesterday a milkman was shot dead while making his daily delivery to a girls' school . . ."

Cross snapped off the radio, refilled their glasses, and they sat on at the table. Mary smoked. The wine dulled the pain in her jaw.

'How did you first come here?'

'Ah.' Cross tipped back his chair. 'The usual way. Cambridge, failed the Foreign Office, taught English for a while here and there. Athens. Beirut. Passed myself off as a specialist in Eng. Lit. and became another of the Council's remittance men. There used to be a lot of us. Not so many now. It's all trade nowadays.'

'Nick used to be – is – a specialist. Metaphysical poets. He had a theory about Herbert: that he was an atheist who invented God to quarrel with because he could not bear a life without faith. I suppose we still do the same; only now it could be Communism or Pacifism. Fascism. Saving the Whale. Something.' Mary took a grape. 'I get the feeling you had that once, and lost it.'

'How acute of you.'

'How do you survive without it?'

'One jogs along.'

'Have you no one at home? Are you like Piper?'

'A nanny in Bognor, on her last legs. I'm rather fond of her, actually.'

Abruptly, the power went as suddenly as it had come on, and they were in candlelight again. Vaguely, Mary thought she should let Rosa know she was safe. If Rosa was still there? Every time she turned her back in this place, it seemed that reality shifted. Even within herself: a woman she did not know was in the process of supplanting nice Mary Lamb everyone likes. Her husband. Cross was saying something about her husband. Oh yes, Nick was steady, Nick was competent – he'd make a good hostage, no doubt, whispered the wicked witch in Mary Lamb.

'And you?' Cross was turning the interrogation on her. He did have the most extraordinary eyes and a face upon which nothing appeared to have been written – not like a boy, but like a man after plastic surgery.

'Oh, me? There's nothing about me.'

Time to go to bed, yes, good idea. Hard day. Mary stood, swayed slightly and Cross caught her arm.

'You,' she said, perhaps a little tipsy, dizzy with wine and pain, wanting to mock, to snatch the mask from him. 'I think you're a secret agent. Who are you working for?'

There was a question between them, of the flesh.

'Myself.'

In the night Mary woke crying. She felt desolate, stripped of everything. Cross came to her bed with a candle. He bent over her and kissed her very gently on her swollen jaw. Like a child in the night, Mary opened her arms.

9

The night crackled with electric storm, though no rain came. Lightning fizzed into the ocean, scorched the mountainside and illumined the blacked-out city with a weird, white daylight. Back-to-back with Joe Porterhouse, and sweating, Rosa grumbled in her sleep. A dog howled a warning. Nancy Prewitt slept peacefully, her face cradled against Nicholas's shoulder. Each time the crack came, Helga the terrorist shivered and closed her eyes. Something had gone wrong. It was not as they had said it would be. No terms agreed. No plane to fly them out. Negotiations suspended.

She drooped. The Milan bank raid had been so simple, clean, a good operation. And now this mess. She should have shot one in the first panic or when the Italian provoked her. Too late now? Or should she act tomorrow, fling them a body? If the old man died in the night she did not know what she would feel and she feared her own grief, as a weakness. Tomorrow they would need food: those disgusting sweet cakes and biscuits were finished. With the power on and off as it was, the little milk left in the refrigerator would turn sour.

The Englishman, Helga saw, was awake. She crouched on her haunches at his feet. They spoke quietly.

'You want a cigarette?'

Nicholas shook his head and gestured to his wired hands. She grunted, lit her own cigarette and held it to his mouth for a puff.

'I think the old man is dying,' she said softly.

'He will if he can't get help.'

'He will anyway, I think.'

'Then let him go in peace?' Their conversation had not woken Nancy but she stirred against his shoulder.

'Why do your governments ignore our demands?'

'Perhaps because we are not important enough? Culture is dispensable.'

'You believe that?'

'No.' Nicholas spoke carefully, picking his way through a mined dialogue. He had seen the girl angry and shrill, using violence without thought. He had observed her concern for Waldemar, but guessed it could not be counted on. Her edginess made her dangerous: it would be foolish to lie in the hope of placating her. Once, no doubt, she was an intelligent, diligent schoolgirl who went home every night to a comfortable house in a tree-lined street, and said Yes, Papa. And then one day she said No, Papa, and went away to kill. That, dimly, he could understand. What bewildered Nicholas more was the discrepancy between her intelligence and the mouthing of those mindless, abusive war-cries.

Now he tried to answer her truthfully. 'No. To be honest, I've never considered the matter. But perhaps culture is a nation's soul? And politicians are not famed for their spiritual sensibilities. I believe if you killed everyone in this room you would rob Europe of something of value. The governments might say there will be other painters, other writers. And we would both be telling the truth. But you'd have done better to go for industrialists or politicians. Families, friends, will want us back, of course – they'll be desperate. But look at the American hostages in Iran –'

The girl bit her nails. Nicholas had noticed this habit of hers before; not just the nails, but the skin around them – it made her hands ugly.

She cut him off. 'The situation is not the same. We offer terms. Like the families of the Americans we want our friends back. These Germans are stubborn and foolish. They must be taught a lesson.' Her voice was clipped again. Nicholas thought wearily: these platitudes of terrorism.

'But you are German.'

'I belong to no country. I belong to an army.'

He sighed and nodded, wondering what did happen between Yes, Papa and No, Papa. Too young for it to be Marcuse, the Free University of Berlin. The wrong set? Drugs? More likely a comfortable home and a Papa who said, No, Helga, once too often; that is, home and family were both branded bourgeois, Fascist. Thinking of his own children, it amazed Nicholas that while protest flourished again this nuclear summer – like the old days of his own marchings – this particular taste for blood-letting had as yet barely touched the English young. It was deadly trippers who came to London to kill and to maim.

'I have a daughter about the same age as you – she looks a bit like you. She's having a baby. May have had it by now.'

'I had an abortion.'

'I'm sorry.'

She shook back her long hair, lit another cigarette and settled more comfortably on the floor, her weight on one arm.

'It was nothing.' She jerked her head in Nancy's direction. 'Your wife is worried about the baby?'

Nicholas let it go. 'Yes.'

'I am sorry I cannot take off the wire. In the morning, perhaps, for a time.'

'Thank you.'

'I think I must tell you – but not the others – there will be no food soon.'

'How soon?'

She shrugged. 'Three days if we ration carefully.'

'But surely your friends out there? If it's a leftist coup?'

'Those bourgeois!'

'Aren't they Marxists?'

'Puppy-dogs of the Kremlin revisionists. They have nothing to do with our world army.' Her moods changed so suddenly. She was quiet for a moment, then looked up again at Nicholas. 'And in all this culture – what is your place?'

'Oh, just a capitalist-imperialist lackey.' He smiled. 'Help with tea-parties like the Congress. I teach. Write a bit.'

'What do you teach and write about?'

'Poetry.'

At first she did not respond. Then she said, 'I used to read poetry once', and her tone was that of a very old woman, speaking of something in her childhood, lost.

When the guard changed and Ali took over while the girl went to rest, Nicholas still could not sleep. He wanted to shift his position, but that would have meant disturbing Nancy. He tried to think of Mary, to picture her, but she appeared against the screen of his mind with face averted. Is that what happens, he wondered, to a comfortable marriage? It becomes as familiar as a house one has lived in for many years and hardly sees any more. That little snap of temper from Mary on their last night (how distant that seemed) – had that been a pointer to a crack through which might be glimpsed the true nature of their marriage? In normal circumstances he would never have given it a second thought; the incident would have been buried beneath the bustle and pleasant rubble of daily life.

Nicholas looked round at his fellow captives. Someone groaned in sleep. By the candle he could see that Gwendell half-slept, trying to stay awake for Waldemar and jerking herself, alarmed, from slumber. Too much time to think – and yet, failing talk, to think was the only distraction from the pain of chafed wrists, aching limbs, hunger and thirst, fear.

Mary. His thoughts ran into shallow sleep. He saw her face turned, in the act of turning, away. She ran and he pursued her, his legs clogged by dream, his mouth stuffed with silence, though he shouted.

Nicholas woke abruptly, a terrible surfacing, to find his mouth dry and Nancy gently clasping his torn wrists, looking up at him.

It was like being back at school. Except for Waldemar, who drifted in and out of the sleep that Nancy said, failing medicine, would be best for him. As for the rest, as each small ration of stale bread, soured milk, sticky and sickly cake was handed out, all watched their neighbour's portion wolfishly. Gwendell discovered that Manzarotti had been hiding a small bar of chocolate and confiscated it. The chocolate became the subject of intense debate: eat it now or save it? Eat half, save half? Deprive Manzarotti entirely of his chocolate? In the end each was given one square, to eat or to save. There was a single square left over. It was finally returned to Manzarotti, but he was sent to Coventry for the rest of the day. The big bear of a sculptor sulked and muttered. Henri Fourges taunted him with his own chocolate. Manzarotti roared. Simon (Non-fiction) Forrester did not want his share. Throughout their ordeal he had hardly spoken and now turned away from them all, huddled in the foetal position of catatonia. When Nicholas – his wrists freed for exercise and use of the now stinking bucket – touched him on the shoulder, Forrester wrenched away from him and covered his head with his hands. Nicholas sighed and continued to circle the room. What day was it? Third? Fourth? He suddenly realised that he must have forgotten his birthday, and he could not remember how old he was.

Mary woke, her jaw aching, struggled up from a cavern of obliterating sleep, so that for a moment, before she opened her eyes, she was to herself nameless, roofless. She reached out and touched flesh, a shoulder.

'Mary?' Cross with no clothes on looked more naked than naked, if that were possible. Like a soldier, after many battles, shedding the armour that has become his carapace. 'I'll get some coffee.'

'No – no, don't go yet.' Remembering, she clung to him. Their love-making last night had been almost accidental, certainly tentative, questioning; now she demanded, coaxed, begged, opened. Her face turned away, she longed to be blotted out and he connived at her violence. Afterwards, they lay back gasping, beached. He drew his forefinger down the wound on her face. Scar tissue was beginning to form beneath the clotted blood. 'We should have got that stitched.'

Mary shook her head. 'No, it doesn't hurt.'

'You've got a black eye.'

'Is it hideous?'

'No.' He reached for his trousers and pulled them on. 'Now I shall make some coffee.'

She called after him, 'Cross? Have you got any cigarettes?'

'American all right?'

'Wherever did you find those?'

His jacket was draped over the back of a chair. He found the lighter. Mary thought, I bet there's no dust in his pockets. Cross bent to light her cigarette.

'I used to smoke. They'll be rather stale, I'm afraid.'

'Why did you stop?'

He reflected. 'Apart from the obvious reasons? It was inconvenient. I mean, not to be free. Like carrying luggage.'

'In case you had to make a bolt for it?' She grinned up at him. 'No, seriously, I mean who is free? There's always something – work, money, home, room, husband, wife, children; friends, obligations? Nannies in Bognor?'

Cross put her coffee cup on the table by the divan. 'The flat's rented. And there are no wives in my cupboards.'

'None?'

He kissed her. 'Not a one.'

The days that followed had a sense of a reality outside reality. Mary told herself: out there Chrissie will have had her baby, life goes on, absurd, wonderful, terrible, tedious. Closer, there is still sniper fire; there are spasmodic street battles, Cross says. Blok's faction have taken the Metropole but Pleiscu still holds the post office and broadcasting station. Nick? She was frightened to think of Nick. When she did, she thought of him in their former, real life, as though he were someone she had known a long time ago.

Of course, it was not so simple. She would be caught out without warning by her anxiety, by her need for news of the Tea Room, by a visceral panic for Chrissie. If she could even telephone Rosa, who must be worrying. But the line was dead and remained so while the radio offered nothing but static, broken only once by a burst of martial music soon cut off. When Cross had been out briefly Mary would look up when he got back but always, before she could frame her question, he shook his head.

So, while Cross made his occasional small excursions, Mary lay on the divan, reading, or watched the shaft of sun touch the icon and withdraw its fire just a little earlier each afternnoon, no more than a minute. In the shadowed kitchen, with its equipment of a man who lives alone (but tidily – he was the tidiest man she had ever known), Mary sliced an aubergine, a red pepper, a courgette, to simmer in oil. Even the main room had no view – only the one small high window which admitted the sun once a day across a neighbouring rooftop. Mary wondered if he would bring back meat. She ran her finger along the spines of books in foreign languages and thought: there has been a discontinuity.

She heard the heavy door below slam shut and went to slide back the bolt. She knew his step by now.

'I was wondering if you were a vegetarian?'

He kissed her and put down a small newspaper parcel.

'No. But there's no meat to be had. The old girl downstairs was lying in wait with some greenish salami, if you fancy it. I think she wants to know what's going on.'

'What *is* going on?'

*

'Doesn't that count as luggage?'

Mary meant the portable cassette player. She could have guessed he would care for music, but would have put him down for Mozart; instead, they made love to the tune of Vivaldi at his most carnal. Or simply lay in the dark with rumbling, thumping old Beethoven.

'You should put a candle on each side of that icon.' She asked lightly, not looking at him, a sudden hunch, 'Were you ever a Catholic?'

'How clever of you. Yes.'

'What happened?'

'I had the opposite of a revelation. God went away. A blinding darkness.'

'On the road to Damascus?'

'At deep field on the school cricket ground, about half past three.'

'You're not joking.'

'No. Nothing happened. It was simply that He wasn't there any more. I was at a Catholic school, so for the next two years, till I left, I pretended. It seemed less tiresome than trying to explain.'

'But I thought once a Catholic . . . doesn't the hound pursue?' In the dark she took his hand. 'I'm sorry. I'm asking too many questions.' Anyhow, she thought, I'm the one with the sense of sin. How will I ever expiate it, if Nick dies?

Mary tried to fold her guilt neatly, tuck it away, lose it among trivia, talk, their love-making – to let the music drown it. One day while Cross was out on one of his forays for food and news (she wished he wouldn't go, because she feared for him, and feared for herself, alone), she turned out her shoulder-bag looking for her notepad and found the amber worry-beads. She quickly thrust them back and made herself busy, cleaning the already spotless rooms. It was a heavy day, grumbling with thunder from the mountains, and by the time Cross returned, Mary was ragged, flopped out. Angry that he should take these risks, angry with herself. She went to the bathroom and dragged a comb through her sticky hair. She brought back two cans of Coke from the kitchen.

'They're warm. The power was off again. We'll have to clear out the fridge.'

He put down his parcel, his prize. 'A melon!'

'I can't think why you live like this. These rooms. It might just as well be a clean prison, a cell.'

'You're tired. It's not good for you, cooped up. I wish you could go out but it's too risky.'

Mary remembered the boy falling against her, the rain of blood. She would have liked to weep or, failing tears, to quarrel. There he was with his stupid melon, his concern, his secrets – this man she hardly knew who was not her husband and had probably saved her life. And she was behaving like a nagging wife, a shrew.

'Oh, Lord,' she said, 'I'm sorry. Forget the damned melon – come to bed. Please. Cross, please love me.'

'I'm frightened every time you go out.'

For three days he didn't go. They stayed in the apartment, and it was a little like a marriage, or one of those dreams that are so intensely real, awakening becomes the fantasy. They both read. Cross worked at his table. Sometimes they slept in the same bed without making love. They shared the few chores, and after a while the old woman downstairs, whose right such jobs were, accepted the situation with a good tip and a snort of disapproval.

Once, Cross was called down to the front door of the house, and came back with a kitten.

'It's all right – not rabid. It was born at the consulate, they gave it to the Council because we had mice. It's never been further than the Council garden and they're closing up now, of course. So the porter brought it round here.'

The kitten stood, awarded each of them an amber stare of scrutiny, and inspected the flat on fastidious, high-stepping paws.

Mary smiled. 'What's its name?'

'Trotsky.'

She nodded. 'Yes, I can see that. Dauntless and impetuous. Probably ruthless too, most cats are.'

Mary found herself becoming absurdly attached to the animal. It set a seal on their domesticity, even if they were only playing house. Mummies and daddies, thought Mary, and remembered a wretched puppy she and her friends had wheeled round in a pram. When reproached, they had felt injured beyond measure: such was the strength of their fantasy. She told Cross about this, lightly.

'I suppose I only remember because my childhood was, relatively, so cloudless. I'm not sure now that was such an advantage.' She sat at Cross's feet in the dusk, the cat on her lap. Cross stroked her hair. They knew they would make love tonight, they would have all night, so there was no hurry. Mary frowned in the gathering darkness, trying to explain. 'I mean – I was brought up by happily-married parents to believe that the world was safe and kind. That leaves one unprepared. And then I was lucky. Strange dogs didn't bite me when I stroked them. It was the other plane that crashed. Two days after my father died, I met Nick. I wanted to write – I could. And then Chrissie and Tim. I suppose I couldn't expect to get away with it for ever. Maybe that was the meaning of the dreams: the Gods saying watch it.'

Hugo Cross was like Nick in his competence, but in no other respect. Nick was so open. His love-making was cheerful. Cross, Mary felt, carried a dark sack of secrets on his shoulder. He made love as though he might drown and bear her with him.

That night Mary lay with her head on his chest. 'And what about you, my phantom lover? Apart from the moment of truth on the cricket ground?'

'Nothing special. Father in the Diplomatic. Not best pleased when I failed the FO.'

'Or when you lapsed?'

'No, that was my mother. He wasn't a Catholic and regarded such matters as women's business, like knitting and babies.

So – four babies, I was the oldest, and I broke her heart. Father actually noticed. You've broken your mother's heart, he said – quite high-flown for him – and then he wouldn't have it spoken of. No appeal allowed. Extraordinary, isn't it, the brutalities the English upper class inflict on their young.'

Mary reached to switch on the light, but he stayed her hand.

Mary's face was nearly healed when Cross came back from his first excursion in three days, and said, 'It's much quieter. We could get you back to the Pension now. If you want to go?'

In the Tea Room, Nicholas said to Nancy, 'The girl thinks you're my wife.'

'How awful for you.' Nancy smiled. There wasn't so much talk now. Everyone was reduced by hunger and the cramped, insanitary conditions. The terrorists had been heard quarrelling in the kitchen – Ali, not so shy after all, arguing with Helga, Helga screeching back, and Hernandes, the peacemaker, trying to calm them. Although the radio was broadcasting again, no one could understand the language. The telephone was still cut off.

Waldemar had not died that night but Nancy thought he might have had a slight stroke. His speech was faint and slurred and he dribbled when they tried to give him liquids. Nancy said, 'I'm not sure, but I think he ought to be propped up.' She and Hernandes did it between them, Gwendell clucking, but then it was found he had soiled himself. Without being asked, Helga cut Nicholas's wrists free, so that he and Hernandes between them could clean up the old man. When they had finished and Hernandes had taken away the bowl and rags, Waldemar caught Nicholas's wrist and whispered something.

'I'm sorry, Waldemar?'

'I said – not much of a Chairman now.'

Gwendell intervened. 'Now, Waldy, no talking. I forbid it absolutely.'

The old man still rested his hand on Nicholas's, who crouched to listen.

'Funny,' he said, then his lids drooped. In stillness, he seemed to be gathering himself, then, almost as though he had thought of a joke, opened bright eyes. 'We spend so much time pretending our affairs are important. It's funny how things get serious without any help at all. I think that is interesting, don't you?'

Nicholas avoided Gwendell's eye. The sight of Waldemar like this was too painful. He sat for a while, the Swede's hand on his, cool and dry, the veins a most delicate tracery. Waldemar wheezed, catching his breath with difficulty, frowning at his own weakness, but determined to speak: 'I fear they will be missing me in Africa. Though I daresay they will find someone who will do. To tell you the truth, I was not looking forward to it.' He smiled, a little ashamed of himself. 'Though every journey matters, even those we would choose not to take. Gwendoline will tell you that.'

Their captors had at last allowed them to use the lavatory in the kitchen block and permitted some daylight – one small square of shutter was allowed open, together with the window, from mid-morning until four o'clock, when the stench of unwashed bodies was at its most appalling. This, thought Nicholas, is the fact of captivity that degrades more than the daily possibility of death: that one smells, that one is either constipated or suffering from dysentery; piles, itches, sores, Nancy's period; Simon Forrester voiding where he crouches, his eyes turned inward upon some horror he will not share but hugs, literally, to himself.

Gwendell was standing at the window. Nicholas came up beside her. Not two hundred yards away on the beach fishermen were mending nets. Two dogs, like children, ran about on the beach, tails waving. The water was the grey of skimmed milk.

Gwendell said, 'He's given in.'

'He's extraordinary. You know, he's thinking of death as another trip. I believe he wants to die to find out what it's like. Though I can't imagine how he'll send back the news.' Nicholas was talking, he knew, as much for his own sake as Gwendell's: to stop himself weeping.

Then Gwendell seemed to brighten. She was almost her old self.

'Oh, that's all arranged! We settled it long ago. Not just Waldy, but some names that might astonish you. There's a little body in Peckham standing by to receive messages. Angora cardigans like knitted cats – you know the type – but utterly reliable, never misses a call.'

For the first time in days, Nicholas laughed. 'You make her sound like a telephonist.'

'Well, so she is in a way.' Gwendell took a deep breath of the sea air. Idly, they watched a large vessel drop anchor well offshore, figures moving on the deck. 'She got a message from Eliot the other week.'

'T.S?'

'George, of course.'

'Does this mean you believe in life after death?' That didn't seem Gwendell somehow.

'Well, out, out like a candle would be such a *waste*, wouldn't it? Everyone is free to make their own arrangements, and I daresay it's as well that most just fade away. But a few of us felt it might be worth a try. We each have a code of our own. Rather like a club, you know, with an ex-directory number.'

Now Nicholas did laugh out loud. 'An élitist immortality!'

'Nothing of the sort,' said Gwendell brusquely. 'I simply don't like to see a good mind thrown away. Besides, one would wish to know what happens next. If anything survives death, it must be curiosity.'

'Not love?'

'Love? Ah, well yes – love.' Gwendell looked weary again. She turned away from the window to take her place again by Waldemar's makeshift bed. First, though, she pressed Nick's hand. 'You are a good man, Nicholas Lamb.'

All day they watched the ship, as long as a street and higher than a house.

'What is it?' asked Helga. 'Is it English?' The terrorists appeared as interested as the captives. Simon Forrester, encouraged by Nancy, had roused himself from his psychotic inertia and shuffled round to the gap in the shutters. All afternoon he watched the ship.

'American,' said Nicholas. 'Aircraft-carrier. We can't afford them any more or only little ones for jump-jets.'

Helga nodded.

That evening, with a curiously ritual solemnity, they shared out the last of the food, both captors and prisoners. They lit extra candles Hernandes had found in the kitchen, and by their light devoured a few dates, a small tub of yoghurt, some stale bread and enough retsina to moisten their lips. Waldemar took nothing but the wine. He was conscious, and smiled on the feast.

No one stood guard – it seemed pointless. The hostages were too weak to make any move.

Hernandes beamed: 'A party!'

They had forgotten Simon Forrester, who bolted to the window and forced open the shutters, making presumably for the beach and the ship. Helga shot him. The carrier stood there, on the water, outlined in lights like a child's picture.

10

'The return of the lamb!' cried Rosa and waved her glass. Mary thought she might be more than a little drunk.

To come back to the Pension was extraordinary, as though none of these things had happened in between, and Mary would just walk in, go up to their room and find Nicholas. Well, he'd say, looking up from his book, his finger on the page to keep the place, and where have you been?

Cross had driven her here in his little yellow Beetle through the back streets, avoiding the promenade. It had been, as he had promised, quiet enough. The city's like a haunted house, Mary had thought: those listening buildings, the glimpse from the corner of the eye of a shadow, a shape. Was that a figure in the alley by the Byzantine church?

'You remember that?' she said, a little shakily. 'You scared me? The place scared me. Everything seemed to go wrong after that. Silly. But the church garbled sense somehow, everything one was sure of.' The whispering gallery, the bird.

'You're sure you want to go back?'

'I think I should. And then I think it doesn't matter much where I am.'

'It matters to me.'

Mary turned to look at him, then away. His profile was unreadable. 'Cross? What do you want from me?'

He changed gears with a screech. Cross's car was the only ill-organised thing about him. Why do I always get involved with tidy men, wondered Mary? They were in sight of the Pension now and, but for the absence of the carnation seller, it was exactly as it had been; frozen in time were the dusty trees, the metal tables with their cheap Martini ashtrays, the fairy lights, even Rosa lolling over a drink. Cross stopped the car.

'You'll be all right now. There's Rosa Treadwell.'

Mary was startled. She had not imagined he would leave her. 'You're not coming with me?'

'Not now. I'll be in touch later.'

Cross sat behind the wheel and watched her walk the fifty yards to the Pension. He had not answered her question. He had taken her in because he had no choice, kept her because she touched him, reached an area of feeling he had believed dead in himself. Love? But she was happily married. Was that what he wanted from her – her happy marriage? The last thing he could have. Driving back, he stopped on an impulse at the Byzantine church. A few bullets had nicked the frontage but it stood, as commanding as ever – once perhaps, the queen of some great piazza, before the muddle of houses closed in on it.

Cross sat for a moment but he could not pray. He walked around the ambulatory. He had the place to himself. 'God?' he whispered, and the name came back to him on his own breath, a susurration. He groaned. Standing in the central octagon, he flung back his head and shouted the Name. But his plea or his challenge was lost, mocked, reduced to the thin cry of a child in the glinting and shadowed intricacies of the dome.

Rosa hugged her, then sat down again and burst into tears. 'Don't you see, Mary Lambsy, you idiot – we thought you were dead!' She blew her nose noisily and took a drink from the bottle on the table. 'Service suspended for the duration. Help yourself. Joe!' she yelled. 'Porty, you slob, where are you? Mary's back!'

Mary sat down and took one of Rosa's Gauloises from the packet on the table. Her hand shook. 'I thought Cross might have told you. I'm sorry – I should have got a message to you.'

'Oh, Mr Sniff – not seen hide nor hair of him. I say, you don't mean you've been consorting! Not you!'

'Hugo Cross saved my life.'

'Ah.' Rosa flopped back, lit one cigarette from another, and kicked off her sandals. 'Sorry, I'm sure. No one's in their right mind at the moment, and it was so awful, thinking of your best friend blown to bits.'

'I thought you'd have got that last plane.'

'Too busy trailing you. Then it seemed time for a drink. Cheer up, Lambsy. Yum! Where did you get that kaftan?'

'It's Cross's.' Mary looked down, surprised to find herself still wearing it. 'Too long for me really. The birds are lovely, aren't they? No news, I suppose?' Rosa shook her head and the tears came again, unchecked. Consoling her, Mary too began to weep, then suddenly Rosa snorted with laughter. 'Old Sniff in a dress! Lordy me!' So then they were both laughing, the two mad Englishwomen in tears of laughter, long after they had forgotten the joke.

There was a ship anchored well out to sea. In the noon-day heat its grey shape shuddered, it seemed on the edge of dissolving.

‘An aircraft carrier,’ said Rosa. ‘American.’ She pushed her binoculars across the table to Mary. ‘I suppose it’s being a presence, like those Russian trawlers and the Rumanian Trade Mission.’

‘Don’t they look funny. All lopsided.’

‘The Rumanians?’

‘Aircraft carriers.’

‘Porty – Mary says your aircraft carrier’s lopsided.’

‘Mary, Mary, quite contrary! And where the hell have you been?’ Porterhouse kissed her wetly on both cheeks.

Rosa was uncharacteristically snappy, Mary thought. ‘She’s been quite all right, Porterhouse, so you can put her down now. Go and do your snooping in some other bar. If you can find one open.’

Mary asked, ‘Can’t they do anything? God knows how many men are on that ship and they just sit there?’

Joe shrugged. ‘Provocation. Too risky.’ Less jauntily than usual he went off, with a wave, ‘Bless you, Mary Lamb,’ he called back, ‘God love you and keep you.’

Mary looked at Rosa. She had been sketching with a stub of charcoal on the big pad she always carried with her, upon which she would record a bleached tree on the seashore, a rock – or, more often, some interior vision, the germ of one of her tree-kings or beaked, ferocious queens. Now Rosa snatched the paper from the pad, screwed it up and threw it to the ground. ‘Have you noticed,’ she said, ‘there aren’t any birds? They’ve all gone, even the mucky little scroungers.’

‘What’s up, Rosa?’

‘You mean apart from everything?’

‘Apart from everything.’

‘Let’s go inside.’

They ate or pretended to eat in the empty dining-room, disdainfully served a leather omelette by the ubiquitous hall-porter and keeper of ferns – the only remaining member of staff, it appeared. Rosa was subdued throughout the meal. Mary waited for coffee to say, ‘Have you and Joe quarrelled?’

Rosa paused. ‘You know how Joe’s always in any hot spot – when anyone’s being bumped off, that sort of thing, coups, people chucking bombs about. And we used to tease him about it. I said he was CIA or something. Well, I think he *is*. Though the phone's cut off, I swear he knew that aircraft carrier was coming before it arrived.'

'You're not joking.'

'It's not funny. There are other things. I think he's in touch with the ship. And he's been very windy since Pleiscu's Reds crawled out from the woodwork. Drinking more. Well, he always did drink.'

'Rosa, I'm sorry, love.'

'I hate this sort of thing, don't you? I hate secrets, espionage, all that. I feel dirty.'

'It's not your fault.'

'I go to bed with him.' Rosa dipped her head and seized Mary's hand. 'Oh Mary, what am I snivelling about, when there's Nick, lovely old Waldemar, even Prewitt and Gwendell, and they might be dead. And yet somehow it's all part of the same thing, same bloody muddle. I don't just mean here. A sort of global pottiness – not to mention acts of God and planes falling out of the sky.' Rosa leaned back and grinned painfully. 'It really does get quite difficult to remember who had the last earthquake or revolution or famine or flood, doesn't it? Then you forget to even try and remember, if you see what I mean. Like telly commercials. You go on watching but your mind switches off. Till something like this.' Rosa blew her nose. 'Sorry, love – I don't usually go on, do I? Come to think of it, I don't think much as a rule about anything.' Rosa looked faintly surprised by her own soul-searchings. 'D'you remember at school? It was always in my reports: Rosa could do better if she applied her mind. That rather sweet soul who did Latin once hit me over the head with Caesar's Gallic Wars and said *Think*! I say, have you really been to bed with Sniff?'

'I wish you'd stop calling him that.' Mary pushed back her chair. 'I'd better go and see if I can have my old room.'

'Oh, I forgot to say: Frogs' Paws has asked us to dinner tonight, so now you're back, that means you too, I'm sure.'

'Who?'

'Frogs' Paws Dobi. Dobbins. The Count. Came slithering

around this morning. Here, of course. It would be too dangerous to go out after dark.'

'I'm not sure I feel like that sort of thing.' Mary stood to go.

For the first time since her return, Mary felt, Rosa really looked at her.

'Mary! My God! Where did you get that scar?'

Mary picked up her shoulder bag. 'Someone kicked me in the face.'

The genteel *tricoteuses* no longer clicked their needles and hissed their gossip in the lobby. Gone, all gone, Mary supposed, to spy and whisper behind shutters of discretion. For them too, she imagined, life must have gone on thus, in the same way, for so long alteration appeared impossible. And then, abruptly, this discontinuity; life wrenched out of shape.

Who was this waiter, now watering his ferns? Why did he stay? He might be the owner of the hotel or perhaps he has no home. Or his home had gone up in one of those explosions. Now he was talking to a small yellow bird, a canary, in its cage above the ferns. That was new. He pressed his lips against the bars and the little bird hopped, cocked its head on one side. He put his finger tip through the bars and very gently stroked its breast.

Mary stood at the desk, wearily. She waited for her key, but felt she must not interrupt this man-bird ceremony. Then he turned and caught her eye, straightened at once, severely.

Mary indicated the bird, offered weakly, '*É bella. Belle.* Pretty bird.'

He understood, smiled stiffly and inclined his head in a slight bow as though he himself had laid the egg that made the bird. He stepped aside for her to inspect the bird and, this ritual done, fetched her key, handed it over, and spoke all the time, quietly, in the language Mary did not understand. But she did grasp that she had been offered a courtesy and was touched, as she had been by the woman scrubbing floors that night waiting for news. 'Thank you,' she said, and thought in what unexpected places consolation can be found.

Lying on her bed, half-dozing, sipping mineral water, she examined her situation and summed it up as both appalling and absurd, She closed her eyes and could not remember Nick's face. She searched her bag wildly, got to her knees to drag their suitcase from under the bed, frantically tossed out the contents, searched pockets, even tore the lining, then slammed the lid in exasperation when still no photograph of him was to be found.

Yet since they came together, why ever should she have brought a photograph? And why did it matter so much now? Perhaps she wanted his picture to kneel to as a penitent; or she believed that his spirit might reside in a photograph.

In the muddle she had made, Mary sat empty-handed, bereft, on the floor. She prayed for Nick to live and longed for Cross, and, like Deborah in her story, in the Land of Contradictions, struggled to grasp how one soul might contain such opposed desires. A metaphysical speculation, she thought wryly: Nick would like that. To her, it felt as though what she had taken to be the essence of her, Mary Lamb, were no such thing at all. Nice Mary, good child, loving wife and mother, kind to dogs and aged parents, had been shouldered aside by some woman not at all nice, the woman who had awaited her in this country of her dreams. And might there be more terrible sisters yet to emerge?

In the contents of her luggage strewn around her, she came across a half bottle of vodka and some pills (for what, she had no idea: Nick's backache? Her menstrual cramps?). She tipped some into her mouth, swallowed, slumped for a time, her cheek resting on the bed; then crawled to the wardrobe mirror. The yellowed glass gave back the picture of a frantic woman with a livid scar – a monster, surely? Mary sobbed and beat her fists against the glass.

It was beautiful and strange – a transformation scene. Dobi had waved his wand in his frog paws and the tired dining-room had become a floating raft of candle-light adrift in the evening. From the same magic box he had summoned a white tablecloth, carnations, and the fern-fancier to wait on them. Dobi had brought his own cook, someone said.

The table was set in such a way that it was reflected by two of the narrow wall-mirrors, creating an illusion of a greater feast, as each mirror reflected not only the table but the other mirror, which, in turn reflected both table and mirror.

Mary was dazzled. She too floated. The pills she had swallowed must, she thought, have been Nick's flying Valium, which he never took but always carried as a talisman. Rosa had made her change and brought her down, and now the Count was saying something, conducting her to her place. Whatever the pills were, they had made her mouth dry. 'I'm sorry?' she said.

Dobi settled her beside him, at the head of the table. His baggy, pale daytime jacket had given way to some kind of greenish, lichen-coloured velvet or cord. In places it was rubbed where the pile had worn away, like a balding animal.

Mary smiled vaguely at the other Marys and the other Dobis in the mirror.

'I cannot regret enough,' said the Count, with his womanish hand, bearing a heavy signet ring, on hers, 'the nature of our last meeting. Although I was merely an interpreter, to have any part in that crude examination. The police!' He shrugged, held up the soft white hands.

Mary nodded. 'This is so beautiful. You have done it all quite beautifully, Count Dobi.'

'All by mirrors.'

Across the table, on Dobi's left, Rosa winked for Mary's benefit. Frogs' paws, she meant, and pimp. 'Well, at least there are no bangs tonight, thank God.'

The Count raised a finger and their glasses were filled. The main course was some unrecognisable but delicious poultry. Mary found that she was astonishingly hungry. She looked down the table and saw Joe Porterhouse booming away. Surely Rosa must be wrong? Real CIA men wore grey suits, rimless spectacles and never drank. Then there was Peter Piper from the Consulate pushing the little bones around his plate. There was one empty place – for Cross?

Still answering Mary's compliment, Sandor Dobi called on Piper, 'It is amazing, is it not, Mr Piper, how quietly one may dine in a revolution? Provided one keeps the shutters closed.'

Piper blushed. 'Oh, absolutely, Dobbins. Keep your head down and carry on.' He looked up thankfully as Hugo Cross came in and took his place next to Mary. 'Eh, Cross?'

'But it's queer,' Rosa put in, 'this lull – like waiting for a balloon to burst.' She took a gulp of her wine and cracked the poultry bones in her teeth. 'Gives me the creeps, frankly.'

'How's Trotsky?' Mary asked Cross, under her breath.

'He's fine.' Cross held her gaze. His sleeve brushed her hand. Mary turned to the Count. She felt bright, in control. She heard her voice in her own ears. 'Lovely,' she said, 'delicious. But what are they? The bones are so small.'

'The little birds? I shoot them on my estate. You know my estate in the hills? One or two little linnets, swallows, any little birds, Missis Lamb. That distresses you, Missis Lamb?'

The nausea was only momentary. No one had overheard their exchange. Between courses, with glasses drained and refilled, there was one of those surges of chatter that make private conversation possible. Rosa was shrieking with laughter at something or nothing. Her cries were joined by Joe Porterhouse's deep bellow. Cross was talking to Peter Piper. Shop, Mary supposed. She turned to face her host.

'Tell me, Count Dobi, is there nothing you can do to help my husband and my friends? You have influence.'

'Ah, in politics, yes, I play a little perhaps.' The Count forked a piece of shudderingly rich gâteau into his mouth, then wiped his lips. He shifted his bulk, let out a breath and looked at Mary with a sideways glance, almost coy, flirtatious. 'But who has influence upon young people such as these terrorists? You know the young – they do as they like.'

'They are *killers*, Count Dobi, not naughty children. They could kill my husband. My friends. But I am speaking of your political friends, those who could act.'

'Alas,' said the Count, gravely, 'in such times as these, who can name his friend?' He bowed his head briefly, then reached for a bunch of fat, black grapes. On his other side, Rosa spoke and he turned away to answer her. Mary sighed, tried to think, remember – something someone had said. Cross, Joe, Peter

Piper? Something about the advantage to some faction of a slaughter in the Tea Room? No, it was gone. Her head was glass. She felt sick. In the mirrors her many faces danced in the candle flames.

'Well, I've got to say, Count Dobbins, this is a feast here,' Joe Porterhouse yelled from the foot of the table. 'I'll drink to you!' You have, thought Mary, too much.

Then, of all people, it was little Piper who called agreement and staggered, unsurely, to his feet, his glass held up before him with precarious steadiness. 'To you, Dobbins! The best parties always!' He wavered, drank, and continued. 'To absent friends!' In the silence that fell all around him, Piper suddenly realised what he had said and was dreadfully sober. 'Oh lord. I'm sorry. I say, I'm very sorry.'

It was at that moment that the world seemed to blow up. Cross thrust Mary under the table, where Rosa had already dived, her hands over her ears.

Only Piper remained on his feet. 'I say!' he announced to the empty table, 'that must be Blok and his merry men. Time for the counter-coup.' Then he too folded very slowly and gently, without hurting himself at all.

The massive explosion came at exactly the second that in the Tea Room Nancy Prewitt slapped Helga's face: a coincidence that startled them both so much neither could move for a minute but stood frozen in shock. Then Helga leaped back and crouched, her rifle at her hip. Nicholas turned to drag Nancy back or to put himself between the two women, but Nancy was too quick for him, brushing him aside to run to Simon Forrester.

When Helga shot him, Forrester had swayed in the window for one awful, eternal moment before he toppled backwards into the room. Ali slammed the shutters to behind him. Nicholas was about to join Nancy at Forrester's side, when he saw that they had nothing to fear from Helga, for the moment at least. She had dropped her aggressive stance and sat with her back to the wall, biting her lip, hands clenched to conceal their trembling. My God, thought Nicholas, she's scared to death.

Nancy said Forrester would be all right. The bullet had only grazed his thigh – it was the fall backwards that had knocked him unconscious, but he was coming round now. After a nervous glance at Helga, Hernandes went to the kitchen and came back with a small but miraculous bottle of iodine and a more or less clean cloth. Forrester opened his eyes and moaned weakly. Nicholas went on to check Waldemar.

'How goes it?'

'You know, for a moment I thought the poet was wrong. One departs not with a whimper but a bang. I am a little disappointed.'

'Fiddle,' said Gwendell, 'you're showing off. I must say, I didn't know that Prewitt girl had it in her. A pointless gesture, of course, possibly dangerous, but it seems to have worked. Fräulein Helga looks quite peaky. Well, Nicholas, what will happen now, do you suppose? Was that bang from the carrier? Have the Americans finally gone mad?'

'No. It came from the town. Listen. They're still shooting.' As he spoke there came the crunch of another explosion, a little further away. Manzarotti had been as shaken as anyone by the abruptly renewed drama outside. He looked up at Nicholas, a black smile on his swarthy face. 'You know, I crossed myself?'

'A very sensible measure, I'd have thought.'

The big man groaned. 'But I am a Marxist!'

Next to him, Fourges fired some rapid, scornful French, ingeniously uncomplimentary, Nicholas gathered, to both Marxism and Christianity, the Catholic Church and the Italian Communist Party in particular. Manzarotti growled back. Through their ordeal the Frenchman and the Italian had developed an almost marital relationship of bickering, reconciliation and reprisal. Nicholas smiled. Odd, and interesting, he thought – the ways in which we find our courage.

Nicholas felt reasonably confident in walking around. Short of panic on the part of the terrorists, their greater danger came, he guessed, from outside.

Perhaps still from Helga? She squatted in the corner, as cautiously he approached her.

'That was a big bang.'

She had her head flung back, her eyes closed, her rifle across her knees. She opened her eyes but did not look directly at Nicholas. 'They have forgotten us.'

He lowered himself beside her. 'Then we are all equal.' In the twilight of the darkened room, he saw his big, sandy and freckled arm beside her thin wrist. He could have made to snatch the weapon and failed and killed them all.

'We still have the guns, the grenades,' she said in a flat voice.

'So you kill us – and then what? Your friends are still in prison. And you may well join them. If you can get out of here yourselves and if you can survive.'

'You think we are idiots, don't you? Mad children. Dangerous maniacs?'

'I don't think you help the world along.'

She did not reply for a moment, then turned to look at him. 'And what kind of a world have you given us?' No shrill polemics now.

'The one we inherited. Better in some ways, worse in others.'

'It seems to us a terrible place, a corrupt place of deadly greed and oppression.'

'And that wretched man of no great significance and no influence at all deserved therefore to be shot?'

She answered sulkily, 'He is one of you.'

Nicholas sighed. From the playground on, that is where the wars are seeded: when someone says You. Us. The moment the individual is overlooked. He was utterly drained, intolerably weary, empty almost, of feeling. His skin prickled with its growth of beard. The girl looked as if she, too, might have come to the end of her strength. Did they take drugs to keep them going, he wondered? Nicholas had a sudden hunch that Forrester was the first person Helga had shot in cold blood and that she had found it more alarming than she expected.

'Forrester will be all right,' he remarked, standing. She shrugged.

'He's nothing. No one. But I am sorry about the old man.'

Just as Nicholas climbed to his feet there was another blast. It shook the Tea Room and brought him to his knees. Entirely instinctively, he flung out his arms to protect the girl, even as he ducked his own head.

This was a full-scale battle, nothing like the earlier skirmishes. Continuing well into the night, it circled them, as a thunderstorm might, backing away to a dull rumble, advancing to crash about their heads. In one lull Nicholas made his way back to Waldemar, Nancy and Gwendell.

'Is he all right?'

'I have no intention,' said the old Swede drily, 'of dying before I know what happens. Have you any idea, Nicholas, who is slaughtering whom?' 'The same as before, I should think, though it seems to have got rougher.'

Nicholas could have sworn this time they were hit, but when he finally opened his eyes and eased himself up cautiously, he saw that, although dust filled the air, tables were overturned and mirrors broken, the building appeared intact. Someone shouted in German and then English, 'The kitchen's gone!'

He felt a hand on his wrist, tugging him down, urgently, and Waldemar hissed painfully, 'You could go now, quickly, by the beach. Go!'

'No point. It's safer in here.'

Towards midnight the clamour ceased. Hernandes found and re-lit the candle. They sat around it, like children at a bonfire. Ali rolled a long cigarette and passed it round. 'Take it,' Helga urged Waldemar, 'it will help,' and held it to his mouth. 'Don't blow it out. Swallow.' Nicholas accepted, as did Fourges and Manzarotti. Forrester was sleeping. Nancy refused but Gwendell took a mighty puff.

'I say, what fun,' she said, 'hashish.'

'You've had it before?' Nicholas grinned.

'Casablanca. '35. What a dear boy you are, Ali.'

They were silent then, sitting out the night, their dazed and weary faces turned to the candle until, as dawn filtered through the shutters, even that small brilliance was extinguished.

Part Three

11

'That was quite a party last night,' Rosa flopped on to Mary's bed. 'The war. Not Dracula's dinner.'

Mary woke painfully, with gummy eyes and a dry mouth. It had been well after midnight when Dobi or someone had finally announced they might safely go to bed. Mary wondered if Rosa had come in to check whether or not Cross was sharing her bed. He wasn't.

'What's going on?'

'I brought you some coffee. That undertaker-waiter chap was brewing in the kitchen. It's foul but hot. There haven't been any more bangs and there are some fairly convincing-looking armoured cars on the prowl. Peter Piper is trotting up and down the corridors. Any moment he's going to cry, 'Oh, my paws and whiskers!'

Rosa's tone was, understandably, tired, but there was also something abrasive about her. Her ebullience had been pricked, her warmth and trust sorely tested. 'Anyhow,' she concluded, 'we're to be kept in. For the duration.'

'For the duration of what?'

'Whatever's going on.'

Mary sighed. 'This is crazy. There's no proper staff. How do we live? What do we eat?'

'Each other, I should think, before this is through. Bags not Dobi.'

'No news of the Tea Room?'

'Do you care?'

Mary grasped one reason, at least, for her friend's sharpness. Rosa – the free and untrammelled, the cheerfully promiscuous – had needed to believe in the Lambs' marriage, in Nicholas-and-Mary, in Mary's virtue. What a powerful element need was in every relationship, she pondered. The new, dry woman she had discovered in herself speculated if that might not be a truer name for love? she wondered how it would be to live without need, to be free.

'Sorry,' said Rosa, in just the same open and anguished way she apologised at school for whacking you on the leg with a hockey stick.

Mary smiled. 'No, I'm sorry,' she said, without having any precise idea what she was sorry for. She felt, in an odd and indefinable way, bereaved.

So the Pension, that had been no more than their base, became their home or prison. Their gaze was turned from the outer brightness to its dim interiors. The fish-tank light and ferny coolness of the lobby where, in the lulls, Mary liked to sit in one of the knitting ladies' basket chairs and watch the waiter feed and talk to his yellow bird. He spoke with the endearments of a man addressing his mistress, and only to the bird did he ever smile – though he seemed willing to share its prettiness with Mary: a privilege, she felt. Once or twice he let it out and, as it made its small flights from its master's hand, around the lobby and back to his wrist, the little bird seemed more of a prisoner than it had in its cage. Although they had no language in common, Mary gathered that the waiter had been made homeless in the bombardment, and with his bird had settled in, for the duration at least, at the Pension. His shoulders sloped. He had a sad face. Precisely and sternly he mimed the shell attack, his waking from sleep, his journey across the city, carrying his birdcage, under fire.

The lobby led in three directions: to the shuttered dining-room, up the stairs, or down into the cellars where they sheltered when the bombardment was at its worst. Mary did not care for the cellars. For the first time in her life she suffered from claustrophobia. She feared these caverns, burial in this dark, cobwebbed tomb. She wondered if that could have been the meaning of her dreams: that in this city she would find her death. Then she needed Cross most desperately, and later in her bed she used him as though only he and only this might hold her from the darkness.

They lay back. Cross said, 'For the first time ever, I've been lonely. Since you left the flat.'

Mary turned on her side and studied him. What a contrast to big-boned sandy Nick he was. She could imagine him as an unfrocked priest. She smiled, a crocodile smile. 'But you're not alone. You with your icon and your Vivaldi and your kaftan. And now you've got Trotsky!'

'Trotsky's got me. I hope the old buzzard downstairs is feeding him. He'll scratch me to death one day. No, I'd never been lonely before – just solitary. That's quite different. Loneliness is an absence.'

'Then why did you send me away?'

'I couldn't afford you.'

She looked away from him and answered, as lightly as she could, 'I know. *Sans bagages*.'

Cross turned her face towards him again and kissed her eyes. 'I love your hair.'

'I hate it. Curly. Unless I have it straightened I can never do anything special with it. Why do you sweat so little? You used to smile in a certain way, you know, and I called you Mr Pussycat. You still do.'

'It comes in useful when you're stuck at dinner between visiting lady novelists sniping for status.'

'Did you go to bed with them like this?'

'Never like this. Not much at all, in fact.' He stood and was dressing.

'You're not going out?'

'I might have to.'

'Be careful.' I couldn't bear that. Mary thought: two dead husbands. Only at that moment did she admit to herself that for several days now, ever since the fighting was renewed and escalated, she had believed that Nicholas must be dead.

Then I am a widow, she thought.

The Pension was very much larger within than one might imagine. For the few days while the street-fighting was at its peak, there was always a lull between two and four. Siesta time, they supposed, and in other circumstances might have been amused. Cross slipped out just once and came back to report that the kitchen had been blown off the Tea Room, but it appeared otherwise intact. The shutters were closed but it would have been risky to make the dash across the road to investigate. The armoured vans had returned. The Metropole had taken a worse bashing. At the Pension they had been lucky – either no one wanted it – well, it was hardly of strategic importance – or the Pension du Parc (a nomenclature they had never been able to take seriously: what park?) was preserved by magic. Perhaps it had a guardian angel?

Mary's worst enemy, after her abrupt intimation of Nick's death, was not so much fear as lethargy. She did not feel inclined to write. She had tried, imagining it might be therapeutic, but the blank pages stared back. Sometimes she helped the canary-man, as she had come to think of him, cook up whatever could be found to eat in the kitchen. There was Joe's poker school in the cellar; surprisingly somehow, Cross had joined this and frequently won. But Mary soon became restless or tired and, to combat the debilitating weariness, she did not go to her room but wandered the corridors of the Pension. Empty now of all but their little company, the canary-man and the scrubbing woman, the place had the waiting, sleeping atmosphere of all hotels out of season. Except that, having been suddenly abandoned, there were signs not so much of departure as of flight: rumpled and unmade beds, even luggage; a straw hat with a flame-coloured ribbon lay on the floor; a wardrobe door hung open; on one bedside table, like a child's picture scrawled in crayon, faded wild poppies and daisies stuck into an empty mineral water bottle, flopped, broken-necked. Mary remembered the children, some seaside holiday, a rented house, a biting wind, sand in the towels and Nick standing above them on a dune, calling; the wind snatched his voice. For a moment Mary felt dizzy and put out her hand to support herself, then she walked on, past a laundry-room, a bathroom, down the ever-darkening corridor.

She opened one door and discovered a small writing-room she had never known to be there. It smelled closed, forgotten. In some other world, how long ago, what adventurous traveller had taken ship from Venice, arrived here and sat at that open escritoire, written home of the long journey, of this country of mountains between European and Hellenic cultures? More likely of mosquitoes and sanitation, she guessed, ran a finger across the leather inset on the surface of the desk, observed ink dried in the pot, a pen with a metal nib, crossed and useless. On impulse she closed the desk, a little gravely, as at some ceremony of death.

And when Deborah came to the last door, there was no Guardian, nor was it locked. She turned the knob.

The unexpected garden – set in a courtyard central to the rest of the building – seemed to Mary extraordinarily beautiful, as though she had been parched and now could drink. A little, it seemed, had been gathered from everywhere: those small blue flowers that, in profusion, drench the formalities of the Alhambra; from Versailles, in miniature, box hedges lined the paths. And then there was that suggestion – the same she had observed in the garden of the Metropole, so long ago, when they first arrived – of something both sweet and rotten, the earth breathing, hotly.

But the fountain was cool. She splashed her face, leaned back against its basin not caring that she would be soaked. A lizard crossed her foot and she jumped back. A hiss from an upstairs window.

'Missis Lamb. It is nothing to fear. A salamander.'

'Count Dobi?'

She could see his bulk, vaguely, above her head, on the sunless side.

'But you are wet, Missis Lamb – you must come up. Please come up and take some tea.'

Ali's marijuana helped. It allayed the hunger and even Nancy Prewitt was persuaded in the end to take her share. While outside the street battle continued, within the Tea Room they spoke quietly and moved little, in an attempt to conserve energy. Helga's eyes were dull. She had ordered Ali and Hernandes to block the passage that had once led to the kitchen with chairs, tables, cushions even, anything they could find, then she appeared to have sunk into apathy.

Nancy whispered to Nicholas, 'It's queer, isn't it? I suppose we're headlines at home. And yet from here it feels as though no one cared.'

Nicholas nodded. 'No doubt they're huffing and puffing. But as things are, it must be difficult for them to know who to huff and puff at.'

'I suppose they'll get my picture from the publishers. No one else has one, since my mother died. You know, I never thought of that? Last time I renewed my passport I put down my publishers as next-of-kin.' She spoke lightly, without self-pity. 'When we – I mean, if we come out of this, I wonder if we'll be changed? I suppose not. What a shame.' Nancy realised what she had said. 'Oh! I only mean for myself, of course.'

'You want to change?'

'I'd like to be braver. You know, I hide from life. I invent it.'

'I think you're very brave.'

She looked proud and surprised, as though he had given her a medal.

They had been twenty-four hours now without food, yet they were plagued by bowel and stomach troubles. The stench was appalling, the lavatory had gone with the kitchen block and flies gathered around the bucket behind the screen. With his fair colouring, Nicholas in particular suffered from the mosquitoes – he scarcely bothered to swat them now. Behind the elegant counter they found one small tap that still, astonishingly, gave them a reluctant and rusty dribble: the cause, perhaps, of their dysentery. Each night, Ali, wearing a black scarf to cover the lower half of his face, like a crazy eastern cowboy, cautiously opened a shutter, crept across the verandah and emptied the contents of the bucket on to the beach. He scoured the bucket as best he could with scoops of sand. Absurd, as Gwendell pointed out forcibly, that the lavatories had been in the kitchen block; she might have been complaining to the management.

From time to time Helga roused herself from her apparent torpor and paced the room, frowning, biting her nails. Waldemar's breathing was shallow – he used hardly any air at all. Nicholas dragged himself the few yards from his place on the floor (how odd – even now territories remained) to join Gwendell keeping watch on the old man. His eyelids fluttered. He groaned, in sleep or coma – it was hard to tell. At his feet Hernandes lay curled, in the deep slumber of the young. 'Y'know,' Gwendell said, 'I asked the boy why. A nice lad. What's he doing here? He didn't know, not a clue. Not like Madam Helga there.'

As if she had caught her whispered name, Helga whirled – not on them however, but on Fourges, who with a stub of pencil had been idly sketching on a pad he carried with him always.

Helga snatched the pad. 'Drawings! There will be no drawings!' she screeched, and tore the paper, trampling it, stamping on it. 'You will not identify us!' She turned, wild, on them all. 'Down – all of you. On your knees. Necks bent. Down!' Hernandes woke, rubbing his eyes, and scuttled away from Waldemar. Ali came to Helga's side. Nicholas bent over Waldemar. 'Get away from him!' Helga screamed. 'He'll go too. We'll kill you all!'

Nicholas raised himself painfully. 'I shouldn't bother,' he said, 'Dr Waldemar is dead.'

Helga put her gun to the nape of Fourges's neck and blew out his brains. It was astonishing how for a moment the Frenchman stayed kneeling, as though in prayer, until quite gently he keeled over sideways, spilling mucus, blood, tissue, brain.

Yes, thought Mary, Rosa's right – Dobi is like a frog; or a priceless and rare toad perhaps, winking and puffing in the pond of his room.

Not room, she realised now, but rooms, divided one from another by screens, hangings, bead curtains. As she closed the door behind her, there was the faraway tinkle of a Chinese wind-bell and the small sound of laughter. Could this be where the Count kept his brothel?

Dobi himself was settled in a high-backed basket chair, with one foot resting on a tapestry foot-stool. He made a gesture of half-raising himself as Mary entered, sank back and indicated a velvet-covered wing chair opposite. He wore what appeared to be a silk pyjama-jacket outside his trousers and some kind of frog-fastening smoking-jacket (unfastened). All he needs, Mary observed to herself, is a fez and a hubble-bubble pipe. An old-fashioned air conditioner whirred somewhere up above (the electricity must have been having one of its spasmodic come-backs) and from time to time Dobi swotted flies with a cane fan, like a carpet-beater.

Mary did not at once sit down, but gazed from the window at the spot by the fountain she had just left.

'All this,' she said. 'I had no idea there was a garden here.'

The Count was watching her closely. 'Ah yes,' he said. 'Before the Metropole – oh, many years ago – before this place was a Pension, it was a private house. One had the best parties here, you know. In that very garden, all through a summer night – and music, foolish ladies, pretty, pretty; travellers from Turkey and the East, from Venice. D'Annunzio once, but that was a long time ago. Another time – though I may be wrong – your countryman, Mr Norman Douglas . . . all of the best, you see, even *les grands pédérastes*. Sometimes I sit here in this chair and I can close my eyes and hear them again. But it is only the fountain.

'But your tea!' he exclaimed, 'you must drink your tea. You would like a towel after your bath in the garden?'

Mary shook her head, but she did sit down. It was a good tea, dark but not acid, served in a tall glass with lemon. She sipped and looked up at Dobi.

'You know everything that happens here or is going to happen.' Drowsiness furred Mary's senses and it was with an effort – like speaking in a dream – that she pressed him. 'Did you have no idea that something was in the air? I can't believe that.'

He sighed, shrugged smilingly. 'If I did, it was in ways you could never prove, Missis Lamb. And even if I did know, and even if I wished to intervene, why do you imagine that I have the power to do so?'

She put down her glass. Her hand shook. She struggled to remember what Hugo Cross had said. 'I know there were members of the Committee who wanted the attention of the West. A slaughter in the Tea Room would have given them that.' He looked at her sharply. Mary spoke slowly, stumbling after words. 'I'd heard of plans to get Blok into power with Western backing. But then the civil war threw everything out, didn't it? Those Americans will never land you know.'

'I believe you write children's stories, Missis Lamb?' Dobi stroked his moustache. 'Perhaps you also have dreams? Most writers do – the food of their fantasies.'

Mary noticed hazily that the foot Dobi rested on a stool was swollen and bandaged: his whole body gave the impression that beneath the skin was a swaddling of flesh bloated and sodden with some dangerous lymphatic fluid.

'Oh well, it looks as though you'll get your man in anyway. So it comes to the same in the end.'

It no longer seemed to matter. Here, in the centre of her dream – for that was where she felt herself to be – in this room looking down on to the garden, with this gross creature regarding her, Mary felt that she had come upon nothing, an obfuscation of purpose, of identity, of all. She eased herself from the chair, steadied herself.

'This was your house, wasn't it?' He nodded. 'It still is?' He nodded again. 'Then why do you hide the fact?'

'No one asked. Why should I reveal what is not asked of me?'

The rattle of firing marked the end of siesta.

In her sleep she thought it was a mouse, something scratching in the wainscot.

'Yes? Who's that? Yes – come in.'

Mary remembered. After the meeting with Dobi, she had looked for Cross, failed to find him, and gone to sleep on her bed fully dressed. Now the knock enquired again and the door opened slightly; Piper's ant-eater nose appeared in the crack.

'Mr Piper? Peter? Please come in.' Mary put her feet to the floor. Piper inserted himself in the room.

'Mrs Lamb.'

Mary rubbed her eyes and pushed her feet into her sandals. 'I've been asleep. What time is it?'

'Time. Ah. Yes.' Piper looked at his wrist, failed to find a watch, then, as if on inspiration, dived into an inner pocket and produced miraculously a Hunter. He shook it. 'I'm terribly afraid it's stopped.'

Before he enquired for butter to put it right, Mary asked, 'What can I do for you, Mr Piper?'

'Yes.' Now he did at last look at her, rather than round. 'Mrs Lamb, I am most terribly sorry to tell you that someone seems to have been thrown out of the Tea Room. That is a body. On the beach.'

Nicholas.

'That is, not necessarily your husband. Not at all.'

As Mary sat, dumb, on the edge of the bed, Rosa's full-throated call came from below, 'Mary! Will you for God's sake come down!'

In the foyer were two armed men. They looked large and threatening in the small lobby among the damp ferns, with their weapons and studded boots, beards and filthy sweat-bands. They must be Blok's men. Only Blok's men wore boots. They were very young and seemed aware of their own incongruity. In an unconscious reflex of fear and pain, Mary put her hand to the scar on her cheek. Yet these boys were not aggressive. This was not a horde.

Rosa turned as Mary appeared on the stairs.

'There's a body, love. They've dumped it outside. We're to look.' Rosa was shaking. 'Sorry I yelled. Shall I go?'

The men were indicating that they could bring it in, but Mary ran past them. Looking at the body on the bench by the Pension wall, she felt nothing, a cold worse than feeling. She heard Rosa gagging.

Piper asked, 'Who is it?'

'Henri Fourges,' said Mary. 'He was a wonderful painter. We didn't know him very well.' Already the flies were beginning to cluster around the unspeakable wound in the dead man's skull. The young fighters stood back uneasily, putting on a show of ease as they shared a rolled cigarette.

'Does no one have a cloth? A coat?'

Peter Piper took off his thin jacket and half-covered Fourges. He shook his head. What to do with him? With foreign nationals of a friendly nation one normally called Fido, or whoever, and that was that. In absence of Fido, the French having skedaddled, one would cable and fly out the corpse. But no cables leaving country and no flights. Couldn't even freeze him, poor fellow, with the power on and off. And certainly in this climate couldn't leave him like that. Bury? Burn? The vice-consul sighed. At the cinema and in fiction they never told you who cleared up afterwards.

None of his business really, he told himself, but Piper had the habit, like a housemaid, of coping with the muddles other people left behind. It went with the job. He indicated to the young men that they might carry the body down to the cellars of the Pension, where at least it wouldn't get blown up. Though he supposed that didn't matter very much any more.

Mary and Rosa clung to each other briefly, then walked back into the Pension. Exhausted, they sank down among the ferns.

'Poor Henri,' said Rosa. 'He was an idiot but I'd've kissed his feet for his work. He shouldn't have died.' She looked plain, her face yellow beneath her tan, her big hands clenched.

Mary nodded. They were quiet. Their temporary estrangement over, it seemed, the two women were taking comfort, as they had so often, in one another's company.

'Violent death –' Mary said '– it's strange. When it's not on the telly, or an accident you can drive past.' She remembered the boy in the square on the way to Hugo's, the blood mingling with her own. 'Even when it began to happen at home, unless you knew anyone involved, it seemed unreal. When there were those bombings in North London – oh, years ago – I was in Chelsea and rang someone in Hampstead. We were talking about a party and in the middle of the conversation there was this thump, and then another, and she said those were bombs and we went on talking about the party.' Mary was exhausted, yet it seemed vital to work something out. She felt herself to be, in the circumstances, grotesquely chattering, and wondered if it might be shock, but she went on, 'You know, until all this happened, we did live on the surface of things, I think. As though nothing were too serious – except perhaps for our work. We invented a world without death or pain. If I believed in a God, I'd say we are now being chastised for our frivolity.'

Rosa grunted. 'Can't find my ciggies.' They sat on and were not at once aware of the quietness. At this time of day there would normally be shell-fire, mortars: ever since the fighting began a cloud of hot dust had hung over the city, reached even indoors, into drawers, cupboards, food, ears, eyes. About seven, the yellow bird in the cage startled Rosa and Mary with a song – just one pure, high, trilling note.

At that moment the two young freedom fighters, or soldiers, or whatever they were, came running back into the Pension, yelling, laughing, calling. Mary caught one by the sleeve, without much hope. 'What is he saying? Your friend? *Qu'est-ce qu'il dit?*'

'*La guerre*!' the boy called, running on, '*la guerre est finie*!'

12

It had been Helga's decision to throw Fourges's body on to the beach, but after the frenzy of the killing she spoke in drained tones, sullenly, 'Now perhaps they will believe us.'

After half an hour she told the rest they could sit again. She's like a wicked child, thought Nicholas, who has locked the grown-ups in and can't think what to do with them. It was very quiet. Manzarotti wept silently and made no attempt to hide his tears.

'Will you throw Dr Waldemar out, too?' Nicholas asked Helga, but she shook her head. 'I am sorry,' she said, 'I had not meant him to die.'

Nicholas covered his face with his hands. It was he who had closed the old man's lids and laid a scarf of Gwendell's over his eyes. With Waldemar – it seemed to Nicholas's tired imagination – goodness and reason had gone out of the world. On a personal level he had lost a gentle and bracing friend who had somehow, among the prickly snares of international cultural politics, preserved his enquiring innocence. After a wearying day of committee in some town far from home, Nicholas would shower, flop on his bed and wait for the tap on the door and Waldemar: 'I say – are you coming down? I have found something *terribly* interesting.' And off they would go, Waldemar striding impatiently on his long stork legs, hair wild, in pursuit of some new and wonderful Snark – anything it might be, from an obscure antiquarian bookseller in Amsterdam to Southend pier – which Waldemar presented as proudly as though he'd conceived it.

With a wary eye on Helga, Nicholas gathered his strength and shuffled the two or three feet that divided him from Gwendell. She was sitting with her eyes closed and did not immediately open them when Nicholas laid his hand on hers. How she had aged, he thought – or rather, she now looked her age: her hands were puffy, her ankles swollen, her strong features blurred as though a hand had been wiped across a painting not yet dry. She opened her eyes.

'Silly old Waldy. He'll miss the end.' Without acknowledging his touch in any other way, she squeezed Nicholas's hand. 'He never could bear that, you know.'

'Yes.'

'Even perfectly frightful books he'd started by mistake – always had to finish them. And now unless our little hen in

Peckham comes up with the goods, he'll never know.'

'Peckham? Oh yes, of course, the medium. But can she operate? I mean, can she operate through the ether, so to speak?' Nicholas was confused. Gwendell appeared not to hear anyway.

'Have you noticed? Bodies always look like botched imitations of their former owners.' Nicholas nodded and thought to himself with surprise how little death he had seen until he came to this place – and such as he had, in bed. If they kill us, he wondered, will Mary get the body? Will Chrissie see it and Tim? He hoped not. Gwendell went on and Nicholas knew the only service he could perform was to listen. 'We had some famous times. Do you have a handkerchief? No, this will do.' She blew her nose loudly into another of her scarves. 'Did you ever see him play tennis?'

'Oh, Lord, yes!' Nicholas couldn't help smiling.

'Absurd! Arms and legs like windmills!'

'Jacques Tati!'

Nicholas could see him now – Quixote of the court, flailing wildly at imaginary tennis balls, long shorts flapping.

He and Gwendell were actually laughing, sobbing with laughter. The others turned towards them wearily, with astonishment. Then they were quiet and, sniffing, Gwendell patted Nicholas's hand. 'Be a good boy. Don't look. I'm going to cry.'

'Normalisation!' Rosa yelled, shouting above the racket of music blaring from loudspeakers, the cheering crowd. She pushed her way between the tables under the Pension trees. 'That's what they call it. I'd say bloody chaos.'

Mary moved up to make room for her on the bench against the wall. It was true, the whole town seemed to have gathered there or were passing through, shouting, chanting, the girls clinging dangerously to the slow-moving armoured vehicles, throwing flowers at the shabby army, giving kisses, thrusting carnations into the barrels of the guns. It was intensely hot – siesta time, but no one slept today; the throng shimmered in the heat, there was the smell of sweat and dust, the sky was white. Rosa puffed, 'The real do's at the Metropole tonight. Blok's supposed to be speaking. The airport may be open by tomorrow.'

'How do you know all this?'

'Joe Slob. Amazing how helpful the CIA can be. And there's a tiddly little British frigate come to join the big American boys. Looks like a tadpole and a shark.' She gasped again and pushed herself up from the bench. 'I'm for a shower if the water's working.' She paused. 'You all right?'

'All right?'

'Oh, nothing.'

Mary knew what she meant, smiled and nodded. 'I'm fine.'

'There must be some news soon.'

'Yes.'

'Your boy-friend's back.'

So I'm still not quite forgiven, thought Mary, and why, indeed, should I be? She sighed, closed her eyes, opened them and found Hugo Cross looking down at her.

'There you are.'

He wore a short-sleeved shirt and, for once, carried the linen jacket slung over his shoulder. He put it down on the bench.

'Trotsky sends his love.' Cross seemed uncomfortable, almost shy. Next to his, not quite touching, Mary's bare arm tingled. Flesh remembers.

'I suppose he'll be going home now we have normalisation. Rosa tells me that's what it is.'

Cross shook his head. 'The Council stays shut till Her Majesty's government recognises the new regime. That is, they wait to see if Humpty Dumpty will fall off the wall.'

'Will he?'

'Depends what happens on the border.'

'You think the Russians really will pounce?'

'They'd have a hard job. There's nothing but mountains up there. You've seen it. Bad tank country. But the Soviets are edgy. There's always the possibility of an airborne assault.' Cross's face was bland as ever, though Mary sensed tension. She felt an urge to touch his hand – both to give and to take comfort – but held back.

'Peter Piper's trying to find out about the Tea Room. He's perked up a bit – I think he's a Blok man. You know, law and order without repression. Autonomy or something.' Mary could hear her own voice, making conversation. The last of the crowd was moving out of the square. Behind them the dancing dust settled. Mary looked away from Cross. She spoke in a low voice. 'I'm sure Nick's dead. I went to see – they've put barricades round the Tea Room now, sandbags, militia with riot helmets and shields. You can't get within a hundred yards.' She traced a pattern with her fingertip in the dust on the table. 'I told you, didn't I? I should've been there, but I was shopping for some amber for his birthday. I still have it. It's supposed to be magical, you know, to protect. I was too late with it.'

Cross gently turned her face towards him. 'And if he were not dead?'

'I should be thankful, of course. Of course I should. But otherwise – I truly don't know.'

Zig-zagging from one pool of shadow to another as he made his way towards them under the trees, Piper puffed and fanned his face with his Panama.

'Mrs Lamb. No one to be seen. Not hide nor hair,' he sighed. 'Everyone's gone to tea.' He brightened. 'You know, that might be a good idea. With lemon?'

Mary nodded. Cross excused himself. He would be leaving the Pension now, going home. 'A few things in my room. I'll see you later.'

The bird-man waiter had been standing a couple of yards from them, Mary now realised, leaning against the wall of the Pension, watching the goings-on in the square. When Piper called him, he came, but at his own pace, took the order and inclined his head, stiffly and gravely. Guests, wars, weather – his attitude implied – might come and go and he would not be astounded. When he brought their glasses of tea a sprig of something green, like mint, floated on top. Mary sniffed appreciatively. Verbena.

'So you had no luck?'

Piper shook his head. 'Office to office I went. Hat in hand. But it seems to be half-day closing. Blok's your man though, Mrs Lamb. He'll see you right.'

'He can't bring my husband back. If Nick's dead.'

'Indeed.' The vice-consul bowed his head, colouring faintly at this mention of anything as crude as death. He took off his spectacles to wipe them and this pleasant woman swam before him. What a muddly thing the world was, Piper reflected; a difficult spot to make much sense of sometimes. Still purblind without his spectacles, he saw the vine as an undefined vision of green and was again in the lush grass of childhood. A little oasis to carry in the head – everyone needed that in the arid climate of life. Since Valerie's death there on the last long leave together, he had quarrelled with England as a child might with its mother for some hurt inflicted elsewhere – in no way her fault, but she must bear the blame. And yet still, self-exiled, Peter Piper could not banish a dream of England. He set his spectacles back on his nose. 'I suppose it's nothing like that any more.'

Mary was startled. 'I'm sorry?'

'England. I was thinking how much England must have changed.'

'Oh. Oh yes, I suppose it has. You'd find it so. One doesn't notice so much, living there. You know – like seeing someone every day.'

'Please forgive me! I do apologise. We were talking about your husband. I did at least establish that there have been no more incidents in the Tea Room, so far as we can tell.'

'We didn't hear them kill Henri Fourges.'

Piper nodded sadly.

'And they must be low on food by now.'

Piper said, 'Well, you know, that might be helpful even. Flush them out, so to speak. The telephone was cut completely when the kitchen was blown off, but tomorrow I think you'll see communications re-established. Like the President before him, Blok wants to stay on terms with the West.' Piper, rather to his surprise, found himself wishing very much that he could help this nice woman – normally he saw people a little vaguely, as at a distance. Mostly, of course, they came to him as problems: stranded tourists, passports lost, rooms double-booked, travellers' cheques stolen. A few more serious matters involving police and drugs, but not often, not in this country. Mary Lamb was saying something.

'I gather you're a Blok man?'

'Oh dear me, no!' Piper put down his glass in alarm. 'We leave political postures to our masters, who have their instructions. Or that's how it was in the old days. I'm a bit of a dodo, you know.'

Mary smiled, and off he went, scuttling from shade to shade, White Rabbit late for a date.

Cross made love to her more gently than usual, gravely, as though he were performing a ritual – taking his leave, perhaps. Afterwards he lay in her for a long time, searched her face, touched her wonderingly.

'What will happen tomorrow?' Mary whispered. He sank back, away.

'The airport will open and the world will come flooding in. All hell. Papers, telephones, emissaries.' Neither mentioned the Tea Room.

Mary looked up at the mosquito net draped from the central ceiling fitting. Like a bridal bower, she thought, whatever that is. I am a monstrous woman. That was something I could never acknowledge to myself while I was with Nick. He believed in goodness, and so he found it – in others, in me. The good woman I was could be wicked only in her stories. Her monsters had angry snouts and stinging tails, and they dwelt in darkness. Cross lives in twilight so I am his fitting witch-wife.

'What are you thinking.'

'That I would stay with you if you wanted me.'

'Whatever happens?'

'Whatever.'

Cross kissed her. 'No. If Nicholas gets out of there, you'll never leave him.'

She shook her head. She didn't know. Later, showering, she wondered if to recognise the serpents in oneself might be to exorcise them. If she had come to the country of her dreams to be lost, that she might be found. Eyes closed, raising her face to the meagre trickle, Mary prayed that Nicholas might live.

They had simply been watching the crowd go by on its way to the Metropole, when they were caught up and carried along – Mary and Cross, Rosa and Joe Porterhouse. The whole air was churned by bells and fireworks cracked the dusk. Mary fought to get out but it was like the stampede charging before a bull-run; all she could do was to reach for Cross and let him snatch her wrist. The other two were relishing the race – Joe, wild enough to be taken for the Lord of Misrule, one broad, hairy arm flung round Rosa's shoulder, the other waving a wine bottle above his head, until the wine foamed to a lather in the bottle and the cork popped out, spilling wine that ran like blood down his face, purpling his lips. Nearer the Metropole there was pressure from in front – a barrier perhaps – so that the running mob was pressed back on itself, yet could not slow its surging momentum. A woman fell, children riding on their fathers' shoulders clutched and squealed in terror, in excitement, wild-eyed. As they rounded the corner to the Metropole the street broadened, there came a stronger thrust from behind and Mary's hand was torn from Cross's grip, she could no longer see him but was borne on by the irresistible wave of humanity. A laughing girl on one side and a boy on the other, joined hands behind her, supporting her, until at last they were jostled into the square before the Metropole.

Lights hidden in the shrubs below were trained on the same balcony where Mary remembered standing that second night of the conference, with Cross, looking down into the rich and somehow sickly vegetation, and out to sea, welcoming the sweet breeze from Italy. The balustrade tonight was hung with flags, music blared from amplifiers, stick-figures gave the triumphant clenched-hands wave and the crowds roared and swayed – Mary now with them, mesmerised – yelled from a single throat as the fireworks soared, cracked and burst above their heads, flowering, blazing, then spilling their bright petals.

The lovers, still beside Mary, embraced, took her arm and pointed, like children, at the sky.

After the racket of the night, the dawn silence was deafening, it pressed against their ears. Their eyes were hot from the shallow sleep they had caught and their dry lips painful. The men looked all the more haggard for their unkempt growths of beard. It would be hard, thought Nicholas, looking round, to distinguish captors from captives. He straightened himself, sat up and rubbed his legs. Helga was watching him.

'They'll starve us out,' he whispered. 'Us too. This isn't England or even Germany.'

'You don't understand,' she said in a dull voice. 'You'll never learn.' Her eyes were hollowed, her cheeks sunken. He saw suddenly how she would look when she was old, if ever she were.

'I could try.'

Almost, he thought for a moment, she was going to soften, break – but she shook her head.

If he could have reached out his hand and touched her. There was a second. But Waldemar's body lay between them. Then one woke and groaned, another coughed.

With his gaze, Nicholas still held Helga's eye.

'Where does it come from? The anger?'

'You gave it to us.'

There was the putter of a boat out to sea.

On the roof, a bird sang: a high, clear, throbbing note.

13

After last night's fling, the city was once more watchful. Mary woke late, confused, from a heavy sleep. She remembered, dressed quickly and splashed her face with water. The little lobby was crowded and she slipped through unnoticed. Rosa was sitting in the deepest shade, groaning and drinking mineral water.

'Have you seen Hugo Cross?'

'No. But here comes Peter the Piper.'

The vice-consul looked flustered. 'Ah, Mrs Lamb, Miss Treadwell – such a bustle! No, I mustn't stop.' But he sat down all the same.

Mary took a sip of Rosa's mineral water and looked round for coffee.

'What's all the fuss in the lobby?'

'Airport open, you see. The press – all kinds of folk. The world and his wife, if they can get a visa with a wink and a nod. But I do most *earnestly* advise you to avoid the press.' Piper mopped the back of his neck with a red spotted handkerchief. Mary noticed that where his collar chafed, he had a heat rash. 'However,' he went on, 'wheels are turning.'

'What wheels?' said Rosa, sharply. 'When do Mary's husband and the rest get out of that damned place?'

'Ah. Yes. Well, now friend Blok is in, London and Italy are talking to Brussels who are talking to Bonn. Then Bonn will talk to Blok and strategy will be agreed upon.'

'What's Brussels got to do with it?'

Rosa clearly made Piper nervous. He pulled his nose.

'Well, you see, this is a *European* affair. Your Conference, I mean.'

He lowered his voice. 'And there is Moscow to consider.'

'*Moscow?*'

'If they decide to tolerate Blok's autonomy.'

'God!' Rosa howled.

Piper blinked and went on rapidly. 'But really, of course,

everything is well underway unofficially. Early this morning the terrorists were supplied with a radio-telephone, food and water. A representative of the German Chancellor and a third-party intermediary are already working closely with Blok's office. Her Majesty's government has issued a firm protest and plea. That is official.'

Rosa opened her mouth and shut it again. Mary remembered what Cross had said – weeks ago, it seemed. 'But the Germans take the hard line, don't they? So there'll be no concessions, officially or unofficially?'

Piper sighed, shook his head. 'Well, I must toddle off. Don't hesitate, Mrs Lamb, anything.'

'What a ridiculous man.'

'He means well. He's out of his depth.'

'Aren't we all.' Rosa glanced sharply at Mary and seemed to make up her mind. 'Come on. One thing he was right about and that was the press. There's nothing you can do, so let's duck out.'

'But the phone – Chrissie, the children.' Mary's protest was half-hearted. Her life, the one that was supposed to be real, of family and work, gossip, books, English weather, was as distant and fragile as a scene glimpsed through a rain-splashed window. At first, she had struggled, thrashing to wake from a dream, arms bound, mouth stuffed, but the sensation she felt now, following Rosa away from the Pension, under the trees, was of one who has ceased to believe that she might ever wake.

Just about to cross the road to the promenade, the two women stepped back before the snub-nosed limousine, cruising the deserted front like a duchess taking the air. So they're back, thought Mary, or they never went.

And the front was not entirely deserted, after all. A couple of Blok's militia patrolled and the newspaper kiosk was open for the first time since the street-fighting broke out. Rosa called to her to come on, but Mary paused to scan the racks.

'The only one was the *New York Times* three days old,' she said. 'Or is it four? I've lost count of time.'

At the end of the promenade furthest from the Tea Room, Rosa, striding ahead, led the way down to a part of the beach

Mary had never seen before, and yet once again – more sharply than for many days – she experienced the sense of recognition. The slippery floor of the little grove of cypress, the heady, resin-scented air, the trailing shadows of the trees, then between warm rocks in the glare of the sun to the perfectly hooped beach: all she had not known was that the face of the figure that turned to her would be that of a friend – Rosa, planted like one of her own statues on the greenish-white sand.

'Rosa, I should go back. I . . .'

'Swim!' Rosa said, and was already stepping out of her clothes. Looking round, Mary saw that they were guarded by rocks, even from the grove. Still she hesitated, then followed Rosa. There was a morning milk-blue skin over the water. Instinctively, they moved through it without fuss, and it stroked their limbs, settled into its nacreous calm in their wake, leaving not a sign that they had passed. There was no horizon. They swam in an element that was both sea and sky.

They lay on the smooth rock to dry. If there had been a god around, in the grove or out to sea, a sporting Zeus, he might have lingered.

Rosa carried sun-oil in the pocket of her smock. She passed it to Mary. 'Olive,' she said. 'I pinched it from the kitchen.'

Mary lay with her eyes closed.

'At first,' she said, 'I thought: but things like this don't happen to people like us. Now I wonder – is it in us? Do we call down these terrible things upon us?'

Rosa yawned and rubbed her stomach. 'You've just realised the world can be a stinking place? And Mary Lamb's not all sugar and spice?'

'Something like that.' She smiled painfully. 'Perhaps I've grasped at last that having an ordered house doesn't mean disorder can't enter. We can even wreck it ourselves.'

Some large vessel must have passed far out to sea. First one wash, then a second, smaller one, curled below them.

They spent several hours at the beach. Rosa produced from her bottomless smock pocket two breakfast rolls and an orange. They ate as voraciously as children, the orange juice running down their chins. Rosa climbed the rocks, barefoot; Mary sat in the sand, then, as the sun rose higher, retreated beneath a shelf of cliff where from the shingle she assembled a necklace shape of coloured stones and convoluted shells. She amused herself arranging and re-arranging them.

Rosa, her long hair loose, let down to her waist, came bounding down and squatted on her haunches in the sand.

'Pretty,' she said. 'But you want the green one there.' She was right.

Mary smiled. 'You remember listening to the sea in a conch shell? The first time, when I was a child, I couldn't believe it. They had to let me take it to bed. I got sand in the sheets.' She leaned back, propping herself on her elbows. 'This is a lovely spot. I feel better. I wish Nick could see it.'

'Those cliffs up there are fantastic. Shapes of men, animals, temples. It made me feel a bit of an idiot, hacking away. Nature's done it better.'

They made pillows of their outer clothes and the newspaper, and slept. In the middle of the day the sun was as hot as ever, though no longer quite so high in the sky. The year was declining. As she closed her eyes, Mary saw that a slight, unfelt air had webbed the surface of the water with silver. Just for the moment, some innocence had been returned to her. Or she had found it in herself.

Mary dreamed of Nick and the children. It was she who woke first, with a feeling of extraordinary happiness. Smiling, she shaded her eyes and called to Rosa, 'Who's that? Is it a man? Can he see us?' She pulled on her dress. Dazzled, she blinked, and saw Hugo Cross make his way from the grove, disappear momentarily between the rocks, then, recognising them, approach more purposefully. She waved. She remembered, and the joy slipped away. Cross did not smile, barely acknowledged Rosa, addressing Mary.

'You'd better come,' he said. 'I've got the car. There's something happening at the Tea Room.'

He strode ahead and Rosa gripped her hand as they ran up the beach.

'No,' Helga said, 'no food,' and knocked the bread from Ali's grasp. She had spoken three times on the telephone, in German, and finally slammed it down. It continued to shrill. She ignored it.

Ali darted to retrieve the bread, stuffing his mouth ravenously, an eye on Helga all the time, a dog expecting to be whipped. And one that might bite too, Nicholas agreed. Hernandes looked nervous and Nancy clutched Nicholas's arm until Helga shrugged. When she feels herself defeated, thought Nicholas, that will be the most dangerous time for us, because then she will have nothing to lose.

'If you starve us,' he said quietly, 'you will have nothing left to bargain with. No one to shoot.'

She bit her lip. 'No food,' she said.

'In that case,' said Gwendell, 'does anyone remember how to pray?'

Cross crouched with Mary and Rosa behind the shelter of the sandbags and all three saw two of the militia step out from behind the barricade. Shirtless, to show they carried no arms, they walked slowly and stiffly across the dusty empty space before the Tea Room. For the same reason – to demonstrate that they were unarmed – they had been obliged to strip to their shorts. Perhaps because it was a uniform they had been forced to shed, they appeared doubly naked and vulnerable. Mary was reminded of Tim's Action Men, years ago – unlike girl dolls, so pathetic without their panoply of war one wanted to put them in pyjamas. Someone else had a similar thought, for in the small knot of wide-eyed people who had collected from the otherwise empty streets a girl laughed, a high sound, sharp, cut off. There was an element of theatre; of farce, as a drab pigeon picked and pecked its way across the stage, oblivious of the drama. In the car Cross had told them that a body was to be handed over.

The three o'clock air held its breath, congealed. Something metal – a weapon – nosed open a shuttered window and the men were still walking towards the Tea Room across the arena. The window was half-open now, the men had nearly arrived. Mary closed her eyes.

When the body had been identified and taken away, to join Henri Fourges in some cold place of death, the small gathering of spectators did not at once disperse but stood on, as though waiting for the next act. Some from respect – the older women crossed themselves – others from unease. As the militia sent them packing with a shout, someone turned, crouched, and flung a stone at the now closed and silent face of the Tea Room.

'Waldemar,' said Rosa, 'damn. Damn.'

'Where did they take him?' Mary wondered, asking Cross.

'To the city mortuary. Blok's reopened it.'

Hugo Cross had smuggled them back into the Pension through a side door. An unnecessary ploy, as it turned out, since the reporters, with the exception of Joe Porterhouse, had run like jackals after the military ambulance. Mary and the rest, meeting Joe on the stairs, had gone to his room: higher than the others Mary had seen, under the roof, with a small, grilled window looking not, as she had expected, on to Dobi's secret garden, but down into some inner yard where the hotel staff, now returned, worked or lounged. A girl with a red scarf tied at the nape of her neck beat a rug on the clothes-line. A boy, passing with a clutch of dead poultry grasped in one hand by the neck, slapped her bottom and ran. She screeched after him, waking a man from his siesta under a fig tree. A scrawny cat was undisturbed. The man, older, with fallen belly and braces over a yellowed vest, scratched his armpit and cursed them all – girl, boy, cat, world.

Mary said, 'At least they didn't throw him out, like Henri.

They didn't shoot him?' She looked around, almost begging. Her voice in her head sounded distant, as though it came from another room.

Joe sprawled on the bed. Cross stood, propped against the shabby wardrobe, hands in pockets, his image in the mirror – because of a chance of light – brighter than his own shadowed shape. Rosa sat on the edge of the bed, knees apart, feet planted.

'Well he's dead. It doesn't make him any less dead. They killed him.'

'He was ill. Gwendell told me.' Mary seemed to need to believe. 'Ulcer. It might have been cancer. And his heart. He might have died any time.' Joe's room smelled male – not just of tobacco and booze, nor even after-shave and similar pungencies, but some deeper, underlying man-smell that every man has of his own. Mary saw Joe rest his hand on Rosa's thigh, Rosa marginally relax. The connections of the flesh. Cross's skin tasted lemony, he hardly sweated. When Nick was away Mary used to go to his clothes cupboard to sniff up his smell – thought herself a fool till she found friends who behaved in the same way and took it for granted. At this improbable moment, as Joe passed round the whisky bottle, it struck her: we have lost touch with, allowed to atrophy, our knowledge of dark and vital powers. So we would fold violence away and lock the door, as though locks could hold it; and we cannot shout, wail for Waldemar. In Northern Europe one bows the head, presses the hand – only the Jews have a ritual, know how to keen, and the Irish, perhaps.

That evening they ate again in the dining-room. Although it was probably safe enough outside now, there was this instinct to take cover. And the night air was sharper than it had been. In any case, there would have been something festive and inappropriate about dining out of doors, with the vine and the fairy-lights and candled intimacy of tables for two.

There had been a brief press conference organised by Peter

Piper, clucking like a hen and pulling his nose. Mary had said she believed that all possible steps were being taken. Yes, she understood the stance of the German government against negotiation. And in the same stiff voice, like a child reciting its lesson, yes, she imagined that her husband would stand up as well as anyone could under such circumstances. Only when she was asked to comment on the deaths of Henri Fourges and Waldemar did Mary find herself unable to speak, her mouth so dry. Then Joe Porterhouse, who had been observing, apparently idly, noisily dispersed his colleagues, herding them in the general direction of the Metropole bar.

It seemed hard now to credit that this was the same room in which Dobi had wrought the transformation scene for his feast.

Beneath the sickly light of two ceiling fittings and a fluorescent tube, the bird-loving waiter served them severely. Simply because they had been thrust together by force of circumstance during the street-fighting did not mean – he implied – that proper rituals were not now to be resumed. He stood on his dignity as a waiter, unbending only for Mary. Her glass he took from the table, frowned and polished it before he set it down again. She smiled her thanks. He gave a stiff little bowing nod and withdrew. They had the bird in common.

Joe sloshed wine into Mary's glass. 'Who's your friend?'

She shook her head. 'Oh, nothing.' She was too tired to explain. She wasn't sure she wanted to, if she could. Before dinner, Cross had told her gently that the terrorists claimed to have explosives planted around the Tea Room. There was no way of proving or disproving this, though it seemed likely to be true.

'Dobi knows,' she had said, startling Cross.

'Whatever d'you mean?'

'He knows everything. I was in his creepy rooms at the back there. I was in the garden. He asked me up.'

'And what did he tell you?'

'Dobi doesn't tell you things – you must know that. Rather like God, I suppose. His purpose not made plain. He accused me of fantasising.'

'Wake up, Dopey.' Rosa jabbed her fork at the lumps of coldish mutton on Mary's plate.

Mary jumped. Cross was watching her. 'Sorry. I was somewhere else. You know, I looked in the *New York Times* today. There was nothing about the Tea Room. It was all about Russian manoeuvres on the border, in Rumania. Will there really be a war? The White House was huffing and puffing. They couldn't be that crazy, could they?'

'The Russians or the Americans?' Rosa yawned. Fed and sleepy, tipsy.

'The world. Who's that over there? They must be Tunbridge Wells.'

Tonight they were not the only diners. Mary indicated an English-looking couple, late middle-aged, the woman merely sipping mineral water and crumbling her bread, the man, stiff-backed, frowning at his plate and dissecting fat from lean. They were not talking.

'Sevenoaks actually,' Rosa said. 'They're Simon Forrester's parents. I met them in the lobby earlier. She's quite sweet but doormat. Though who wouldn't be crushed? I think she'd like to talk to us but he won't let her.'

Mary said, 'The poor woman. I shouldn't think you'd ever get over that, would you – a child. That must be the worst.'

'Mary, Mary, sweet darling heart,' said Joe, and kissed her. This time she didn't mind. She smiled and played with her food, let the others talk on (Cross didn't speak at all though, not at all), tried to remember what Simon Forrester looked like, allowed her gaze to wander over the Forresters, to a crack in the ceiling, a sticky fly-paper, one of the black and white floor tiles chipped, then across the empty tables to the unshuttered windows which framed – with the fairy-lights switched off – an utter darkness in which it was hard to believe that people talked, were silent, wept, slept, or that even a spark might glow.

Nicholas moistened Gwendell's lips with the rust-coloured tap water.

'Try to drink some.' He held the cup to her mouth, tipped it a little and she swallowed.

'When I was a gal –' She had difficulty speaking, took another sip and opened her eyes. 'When I was a gal, could go weeks without food.' Her speech was slurred and Nicholas had to bend closer to catch her words. She wagged her finger at him. 'Not true about camels y'know.'

'Camels?'

'Fat in the humps. Not water. Fat.'

'You shouldn't talk, Gwendell.'

'No talking where Waldy's gone, eh?'

Nicholas lowered himself to the ground beside her, passing the cup of water to Nancy. They had all agreed – the terrorists too – that Waldemar's corpse must be handed over. The heat. The flies. The stink. Helga had made the arrangement on the telephone, and it had been carried out decently, so far as such a thing can be decently done.

He took Gwendell's hand and closed his eyes.

'Do you know,' she said, 'there is the most *interesting* train? I had been planning to take it, now the Chinese are behaving more sensibly. The Central Kingdom Express, from Hung Hom via Canton, Shanghai, Nanking, Luoyang, Xian, Peking, Ulan Bator. No – Datong before Ulan Bator. Then Irkutsk, Moscow, Berlin and Paris. Forty-two days to Victoria Station – or the other way round, of course.'

'What a lovely name,' murmured Nancy. 'Central Kingdom Express. It sounds like Dante. *Paradiso*, of course.'

'Quite infernal in places,' said Gwendell. 'One would need stamina, Lomotil, laxatives, a hundred paperbacks and plenty of knitting. Or a companion with whom to play word games. But at my age – so many good companions gone.' She grunted. 'You know what you regret? Journeys never taken. No one can take all the journeys. What a pity.'

Journeys never taken, thought Nicholas: and there are those of the heart too. Just for a moment in this ordeal I imagined that Nancy – what did I imagine? An absence of Mary, that was all. His eyes felt crusted. To think was exhausting, to sleep impossible, except in a shallow falling out of consciousness, the waking worse than not to have slept at all.

But the boys and Helga were clearly as exhausted. Ali had quarrelled violently with Helga this morning and now, without warning, Hernandes – whose good spirits had given them all a wafer of hope – leaped from his crouched position and ran from wall to wall, beating his head and crashing his balled fists. Blood ran from his nose. Simon Forrester, curled in his foetal attitude, watched wide-eyed, like a child whose parents have run mad.

It was hard for Ali and Nicholas to hold Hernandes between them. At first he fought, then, even when he had given in, trembled uncontrollably, yelling in English at Helga who stood, uncertain, as startled as anyone, 'It didn't work! You told us to do it and it didn't work! It's spoiled!'

A few days ago, Helga would have slapped his face. Now she regarded him blankly until, still blubbering, he subsided. Nancy Prewitt dragged herself across to the boy, wiped his eyes and took his hands.

Nicholas went to the tap for water and squatted for the moment next to Helga. He offered her water. She shook her head. He spoke quietly, after reflection.

'Just then I could have got one of Hernandes's grenades, you know.'

'Why didn't you?'

He shifted his position. 'Even if I knew how to handle the things, I didn't want any of us to die. I've felt that since Waldemar, haven't you? That the battle – at least inside these walls – is over. I was never in any war, you know. Just missed Korea. Haven't looked, I suppose. Tucked up with my books. Haven't noticed we're all in a war all the time. We no longer have to look for it. It comes to us any day when we least expect it.'

Helga pushed back her hair. 'Do you know, when you get in this sort of thing, you can't stop? And you get in for all kinds of reasons. Hernandes is a schoolboy who was bored by lessons. Ali's people have suffered great wrong.'

'You?'

'I was happy when I was a child – the pretty girl, who was clever too, and would go to the university and marry the good lawyer. And then I found that people were telling me lies. I saw I was in a prison, a cage my family had made and German history had made; my good lawyer would be just another fat German. I had his child aborted and went away from him. I belong to these people: everywhere I have brothers and sisters and husbands. I tell your friends we have wired the place for explosives: that is a lie. Hernandes made a mess of that. They say they will bring our friends on an aircraft and we may go with them. Another lie. Even if they bring our friends, they will kill us at the airport.'

'What will you do?'

She shook her head. 'Hernandes was right. It is spoiled.'

The girl appeared so disconsolate, Nicholas was stirred by some absurd impulse to take her hand. The bones felt thin and bird-brittle. Twenty-five years ago, he wondered, would he have joined them? He thought no, but he would have understood. Her hand lay passive in his. His lids drooped.

'Rest,' he said.

'Missis Lamb'. Mary had placed a call to Chrissie's number but without much hope. Then the waiter, in one of his many roles, as hall-porter, had indicated that a connection had at last been made. When she reached the telephone in the lobby he was before her, holding the receiver to hand it to her as though conferring a gift.

Mary ran back to the table, breathless. 'Chrissie – the baby! A boy – they're both fine. I couldn't hear much, and then we were cut off, but it was Chrissie herself. It was a week ago and we didn't know!'

'Oh Mary, oh love!' Rosa hugged her, Joe too, while Cross was talking to the waiter, who nodded, left the room and returned with two bottles of champagne. Opening them, and filling Mary's glass first, he poured as if he were giving the most precious gift in the world. Behind him came the scrubbing woman – normally he would have clucked her away but today he stood back benevolently, while the woman shyly pressed into Mary's hands a bunch of the inevitable carnations. Mary was undone now, laughing, crying. If only Nick. She pointed to the Forresters and the bottle, the waiter nodded and crossed to their table. Studiously they had been trying to ignore the wild goings-on across the room, but were now obliged to recognise the spontaneous party. The husband raised his glass and made a token bow of the head to Mary.

Rosa was attempting to pour the champagne from the bottle into Joe's open mouth. Mary sat, the ragged carnations in her lap, and looked up at Cross. She plucked one of the carnations from the bunch and stuck it in his buttonhole. Unsmiling, he caught her fingers and kissed them. 'I must go,' he said. 'I'm glad for you.' She saw him cross the lighted window, then the darkness closed behind him.

'Hey, Grandma, wake up.'

'Sorry, Joe. Miles away.' She swallowed her champagne – rather sweet, honey-tasting, as if from bee not grape. 'I think I'll go up.'

She had reached the lobby when she felt a light touch on her arm.

'You've dropped your lovely flowers.'

Mrs Forrester was holding the carnations awkwardly; their pink clashed with her ugly, orange-splashed dress, of sunflowers on black silk. A hopeless dress, thought Mary irrelevantly – her mind muzzy with drink, exhaustion, excitement, apprehension – an irredeemable one, even the cut harsh on this bony woman. Mrs Forrester seemed not to know how to hand over the flowers. She spoke nervously and rapidly.

'My dear, I am so happy about your grandson. That must be such a joy. Herbert and I.' Her voice trailed off. Mary thought, how can I answer her? The back of her husband's stiff red neck could be seen through the door, disapproving.

'Thank you. That is very kind.'

Mrs Forrester looked round, at the ferns, the bird. Mary could see her, in some other world, happy in this place, knitting gentle gossip, exchanging family photographs. Oh God, she thought: Simon. She hardly knew him. Mrs Forrester's mind had been off on the same track.

'He's our only one,' she said shyly, then checked herself in horror. 'But of course – your husband! How clumsy of me. I'm sorry. So sorry.' She turned away, appalled, and then back. 'Your flowers. Please forgive me. Mr Forrester always says I go where I'm not wanted.'

Mary hesitated. In her anxiety, the other woman had dropped half the dusty carnations. Mary bent quickly to pick them up, gathered the whole bunch together and laid them in Mrs Forrester's arms. 'Please,' she said, 'keep them. You've been so kind.' Then she ran up the stairs.

14

Dobi sat by his window. His foot pained him and he felt fretful in a way he could neither define nor ease. He pulled his moustaches and observed that the sun must be a little lower in the sky – it no longer fingered the fountains at midday and by three o'clock shadow had taken more than half the garden. Colour had drained from his life also. The games were no longer so amusing. He drowsed, his head drooped, and the secret garden was peopled by the laughing dead.

Helga announced: 'The aircraft arrives this evening. We may speak to our comrades on the radio telephone. At nine o'clock tonight we are to have safe conduct to the airport. It will be necessary for you to accompany us as hostages to Algiers, where you will be freed and flown home. This is a victory for the world revolution.'

She sounded incongruously like a tired air hostess, and for a moment, still dazed from a night of discomfort and sleeplessness, they hardly grasped what she said. It was Gwendell who spoke first: 'Well. Then we'd better pack.'

A crack of uneasy laughter, then Manzarotti wept and his tears released the others from their shock. Shakily, they smiled and embraced, and then looked away from one another, appalled by the reflection of their own faces in their fellow prisoners'. All the men – except for Simon Forrester, whose chin wore the tenderest down – had a week's untidy growth of beard. Their faces were honed, gaunt, their bodies ulcerated and stung. Legs were as uncertain as reeds and ankles swollen. For the first time, contemplating release, they were ashamed before each other.

Helga's decision to resume contact with the outside world had come abruptly. In the night she had spoken in German on the radio telephone. This morning she had accepted a chemical toilet, food and fresh water. A triumph, Nicholas supposed, yet she had the air of someone who had lost rather than won. She slumped, turned in on herself, chewing her nails, while the others ate a little of the food and sipped the water. Several found the food too much for their shrunken stomachs.

'You don't trust them?' Nicholas asked. Helga shrugged. Ali and Hernandes were now positively cocky, sprucing themselves, cleaning their rifles.

'The idiots.'

'What made you change your mind?'

'This was a bad operation. Ill-prepared. They would storm us soon. So I take the risk.' She jerked her rifle in Nancy's direction. 'That is not your wife?'

'No.'

'But you have a wife.'

'Out there. I hope.'

'Oh yes. The coup.' She turned her head wearily, towards him. 'You know the Jews killed all of Ali's family? He was at Camp Khayat. They shelled his village, the houses, the infant school. The babies.'

In the mirrors of the Tea Room – crazed and splintered by the blast from the explosions – the hostages cautiously regarded themselves. Manzarotti became manic. He broke Nancy's comb in his tangled beard, yelled with laughter, danced like a bear. The rest were not sure how to react. They were elated, confused, between worlds.

In the middle of the day Nicholas stood with his back to the wall, his head craned to see out of a raised slat in the blind. There was a square of implacable sun, a white and staring mat walled by fortified barricades, black. He guessed there would be snipers in the top floor of the old Casino opposite but the windows were blank rectangles, secret, watching. It looked like a world unpeopled, yet there was a tension in the relation between solid objects and light, as though signals were exchanged. Walls were pock-marked by the street-fighting. The house next to the Casino had gone, leaving an iron bedstead on what had been the first floor, precariously balanced on buckled girders.

Nancy came up beside him.

'I can't get Simon to understand. That we'll be free. I'm not sure he can take it: leaving here, I mean, the flight if there is one.'

'We'll manage.'

They went on talking, but if there had been an idea of more than talk between them, the hope of freedom dispelled it. Nancy was not self-deceiving. She kissed Nicholas lightly on the cheek and went back to Simon. She took his hands and talked to him, crouched, then sat down beside him, still talking, coaxing.

Heat. Words like moths in Nicholas's head. Midi. Mezzogiorno. The heavy iron hand of the sun. Gwendell has a fly on her nose. Breathe softly, still, wait. A dream of Mary, pregnant, standing on a beach, offering fruit – a peach? a pear? He woke to see Helga sitting on one of those absurd white iron benches, her head resting against the wall. Her Che T-shirt was soaked with sweat between her small breasts and her hair hung lank. For the first time Nicholas allowed himself to think: I might see Chrissie again.

'Why do you wear that chain round your ankle? Is it gold?'

'A boy. He's dead. Pretend gold.'

'Was he a terrorist?'

'A guerrilla.' Helga corrected him almost in the tone of a schoolteacher, automatically, without reproach. She sat with her knees drawn up to her chin, her ear to the wall, listening. 'I can hear the sea. You know when you listen to a shell? Like that.'

'How did your friend die?'

'Mogadishu.' She spoke like a veteran of old and famous battles. Nicholas tried to imagine her life, what drove her. A true cause or repining restlessness? His earlier guess as to her first impulse had been more or less right – but to carry on? He felt a foolish urge to embrace her – as he had taken her hand not so long ago – as he would once have held Chrissie when she cried in the night. He smiled grimly to himself. Going soft on killers, eh? A little sadness for one girl who bites her nails and the flesh from the sides of her fingers. She was talking. As she talked Helga's face cleared, her expression lifted: 'That boy – he was funny, you know. He made me laugh. Clown. He reminded me of a cousin when I was young, who never got into trouble because he made the grown-ups laugh. We hated him, of course, but I adored him too.'

Nicholas shifted his bulk. He caught Gwendell watching him, a glint in her eye. Helga said, 'Do you love the woman who is not your wife?' He was taken aback for a moment.

'Nancy? No. But I know her better.' He said lightly, 'You won't miss all that one day: family? children?'

She looked at him sideways, her hair falling back from her face, her chin still resting on her knees, and for a second Nicholas could almost believe that she might be teasing him: 'How could I? I have the revolution.'

'That is your family?'

'Yes.' She thought, raised her chin and corrected herself.

'No. More like a stern father. As people used to think of God perhaps, the old God. Within it, you know, we are individuals: brave, frightened, weak, strong, heroes, idiots. We don't spend all our time plotting, killing, any more than the Fascist torturers of your world give all their minds and souls to the refinement of the electrode. The difference between them and us is that they go home at night. I think sometimes I would like that.'

Nicholas shook his head. At the best, he saw them all as suicides. Useless to point out, he supposed, that there were Fascists in their world, too. Impossible too to forget – though for a moment he nearly had – that this old-young girl had killed Henri Fourges; and, indirectly, Waldemar.

Quite suddenly Nicholas was weary of this dialogue, of all dialogue, of the talk, of the dangerous silences, of the tugs to the emotions, the battleground this time had made of him. Standing, he saw his reflection surrealistically shattered in the mirrors, half-a-dozen selves. He wondered if they would die tonight. His beard itched.

'Is it true or a trap?' Mary was sitting in the lobby. One of Blok's militia had just left.

'It could be both,' Cross said. 'The Germans may be bringing the prisoners. At the same time they may be planning to grab the terrorists – either at the airport or outside the Tea Room.'

Mary sagged. All this time pretending one was not waiting for the explosion and now good news that might be as bad. She pondered. Mrs Forrester was in the lobby too, sitting on the edge of one of the cane chairs, her hands fiddling with the white plastic bag in her lap, twitching at her cardigan, touching her throat. Her husband paced outside, smoking a pipe, marching up and down, tapping his cane, a stern profile. Cross couldn't stay – the Council was opening up again; Rosa and Joe were still in bed.

Mr Forrester marched indoors and upstairs. His wife made a half movement to rise and then sat back.

'It is difficult,' she offered shyly, 'the waiting. But, of course, you have been waiting much longer. We had hoped. But it seems to be all we can do. To be here.'

'Would you like to walk?'

On the promenade Mrs Forrester seemed a little less nervous – as an Englishwoman, she knew where she was, walking at the seaside. Mary had thought it best to avoid the streets, with their marks of battle. A little colour came into the other woman's cheeks and she paused, her hand on the rail, looking down on to the beach.

'We used to love the seaside, Simon and I. His father never had much time for it. Men don't, do they?'

Mary smiled, shook her head.

'Do you know Simon well?'

'Not very.' Perhaps not mention Gwendell, Mary judged – even if there had been any truth in it. That gossip: it all seemed so far away, a story of another life. Mary recalled Simon's latest book: yet another Bloomsbury biography, rapturously reviewed and almost universally unread. She had left her copy somewhere – on the plane? 'But we all think a lot of his work.' What am I doing, she thought, patronising this woman with my pity?

They strolled on. There was little traffic. A boy on a bicycle. The sea was greyer today, fussing at the shingle, the breeze stronger. Mrs Forrester pointed to a turning off the front.

'Where does that lead?'

'To the town. There's a Byzantine church.' Mary added reluctantly, 'We could go back that way?'

Just as they were turning into the narrow street that led behind the Pension to the church the familiar Mercedes nosed out. From somewhere above or behind the women, a missile was thrown, striking the limousine, which immediately accelerated. Mary caught Mrs Forrester by the arm and pulled her into the shelter of a doorway. 'Those are Rumanians,' she said, 'supposed to be a trade mission but not over-popular.' She looked up at the shuttered windows and after the disappearing Mercedes, then laughed shakily. 'It was an egg. Only an egg. Look – you can see.'

'I should like to see the church,' said Mrs Forrester, with surprising firmness. She had not been upset by the egg. Quite briskly, she strode out.

There had been considerable damage round here. Mary was confused by vanished landmarks. No washerwoman cried and gossiped now – instead there was a silence pierced by a toffee-eyed boy who appeared suddenly from among the rubble to pursue them with the familiar cry, 'Missis-missis!' Mary walked faster, hoping that the church might be locked or gone. But only the door had been blasted from its hinges. She remembered the terror she had felt here, the bird in the dome, the whispering ambulatory, and nearly cried out as something furry brushed her ankle.

'The poor things,' said Mrs Forrester, and now Mary saw: the stray cats of war had made this their place. Someone must have fed them, if only a little; it might have been kinder to let them die. The smell was appalling, but, undeterred, Mrs Forrester found a stool, knelt and prayed. Mary sat beside her stiffly, hands clenched, sensing at the nape of her neck the alien and anguished figures in the shadows of the ambulatory. No God here, she thought, or if there is, none I could speak with. Waiting for Mrs Forrester – her hands joined like a good child at bedtime, her head bowed to whatever power it was that sulked here – finally Mary gave in. Weariness, if nothing else, pressed her to her knees, and once on her knees, she prayed, surprised that she could remember how.

The radio telephone had been set up in the same police station Mary had visited to so little purpose when all this began. The man behind the desk was more correct, a little smarter, conscious of the presence of the German emissary and Dutch intermediary. The room was cleaner, the windows were taped against blast, there were armed guards posted at the doors. Draza Pleiscu had vanished but his men were held, Mary had heard, in the cells below, awaiting trial. There were rumours of torture. The new policeman spoke English and French but Peter Piper hovered. Cross was there.

Mary sat in this room of men. She was to speak to Nick to identify him to prove that the rest of the hostages lived.

'Now Mrs Lamb.'

'Nick?'

His voice seemed to come from a great distance. He was fine. The rest were all right. They were cut off. Mary still held the receiver. Her hand shook. She looked up and met Cross's eye, reading pain in his face.

'Yes. Yes, that was my husband. He says they are all well.'

Someone took the receiver from her hand. There was something she meant to say to Cross, but she was to go, she understood, she was to be taken to the Pension. She looked back for Cross but Peter Piper fussed her into the military car.

In the Tea Room, about six o'clock, they roused from the stupor of the afternoon; Nicholas handed the earphones to Helga and looked round. They had the appearance of travellers waking crumpled and weary from an overnight journey in the same carriage. Helga was speaking in German to her friends on the aircraft, he assumed. Nancy Prewitt straightened her clothes as well as she could, persuaded Simon Forrester to take a little to eat and drink, and then washed first his hands and then his face with a cloth wet from the tap: she worked with the assiduousness of a cat grooming a kitten.

Gwendell seemed to have perked up a little. 'Another journey, eh?'

Nicholas scratching his chin. 'If we make it.'

'Either way a trip.'

'And if we're dead?'

'Then we shall find out, shall we not, if the sorceress of Peckham was right. Would you mind looking away and passing me the bowl? I really must wash my teeth.' That done, the Dame dabbed her mouth. 'I do believe that Italian is telling his beads. One had heard he was a Marxist.' Nancy had joined them now, and was squatting like a girl, her feet tucked under her. Gwendell went on, 'When I was a gal in India, we travelled with ice in the carriage, you know. It never melted all the way.

And at every station they sent on the food we had ordered. It was quite delicious. And in the hills it was heaven. When I was young I used to believe that the after-life might be Simla.' She coughed, raspingly, and Nicholas fetched her a cup of water, not from the tap but from the mineral water sent in.

Nancy was saying, 'I believed in God until I was twenty-four, when my puppy was run over. It took it all night to die. It thought I was God and I had let this happen. All the terrible things in the world – but perhaps you have to stay up all night with a meaningless death to grasp the fact that He is either dead Himself or a mad executioner.'

Delivered of this speech – enormously long for her – Nancy blushed and ducked her head. So, with the hope of an end to their ordeal, they were tentatively returning to their former selves. Not quite yet and not altogether, but there were signs.

Gwendell looked at Nancy with astonishment, as though a rabbit had burst into grand opera. She recovered herself. Her tone was crisp.

'I would say more, you know, that if He is there, He is a despairing parent who has done the best for His children and they have let Him down.' She turned to Nicholas. 'And how was Mary?'

'Hard to tell. Not the best circumstances for an intimate conversation. I think she wasn't alone.'

Gwendell nodded. 'Dear girl.'

There was a cheer from the other side of the room where Helga had finished speaking. Hernandes, more than restored to his former cheerfulness, embraced a tearful Ali and announced to all at large, 'Our friends! Our comrades are safe – they are in the plane. We shall all be free!'

First Nancy clapped her hands together, then Manzarotti laughed and smacked a great kiss on her cheek. Even Simon Forrester smiled. There was a feeling that these were not captors and prisoners but just for a moment, all one, joined in a single triumph. Nicholas glanced at Helga. She was expressionless.

'Isn't it silly,' said Nancy, 'I think I'll almost miss them.'

'If we could be there –' Mrs Forrester dropped a stitch. Mary nodded. No exceptions could be made to the curfew. A black and white television had been set up in the dining-room and they sat around it, uncomfortable on the hard chairs. Her waiter – as she had begun to think of him – stood behind them, against the wall. He stepped forward, frowned, and adjusted the set. A man's face dissolved and was reformed. There was a shot of girls dancing, in peasant dress of full skirt, pinafore, frilled white blouse and laced bolero. A small child was presenting flowers to a man who must be Blok. She climbed some stairs and tripped, still clutching the flowers. There was a beam on the wide, homely face of the President as he bent to help her, then raised her up to the level of his shoulder.

'At least the curfew keeps the press holed up at the Metropole,' Mary said, then, although she was expecting it, stiffened as the inevitable scene came up. She felt Rosa clutch her hand. There was the Tea Room, with its shutters and absurd minarets, blank-faced, giving away nothing in the grainy monochrome of mid-evening. A gasp from Mrs Forrester and she dabbed her nose – already pink – with an inadequate tissue. Beside her, her husband, the man of granite, cleared his throat and stared ahead, unflinching before the screen.

The Tea Room looked simply as though it had been closed for the season. The square before it was empty and the only sign of a human presence was the black finger of a weapon at the bottom of the picture – caught as the cameraman crouched behind the barricade, shoulder to shoulder with the militia.

'What's that?' Mrs Forrester touched her husband's sleeve, then withdrew her hand sharply and half laughed, half sobbed, as a small dog crossed the square from the Casino side, sniffed at one of the ornate lamps outside the Tea Room, cocked a stiff leg and walked out of the picture. Briefly, the scene changed to the airport and a furry image of the Lufthansa jet. The newsreader spoke, then up came Blok again, solemn this time, addressing a meeting. Mary groaned. When he called earlier this evening, Cross had explained the rising fear of Russian intervention. He looked tired. He kissed her on the cheek and awkwardly pressed into her hands a rectangular brown paper parcel, then he was gone. She had a feeling she might not see him again.

It was nine o'clock – that moment of tenuous softness rather than true dusk that comes in southern countries before the dark. They saw the armoured car swing into the road outside the Tea Room. It was unreal. It was television. Gwendell stepped out first, supported by Nicholas. Both seemed to have difficulty walking. Behind them, carrying her automatic, came the girl. Suddenly there was a rattle of firing and Nicholas, stooping to help Gwendell into the car, looked back over his shoulder. The girl appeared merely to have lost her balance for a moment, but then she staggered and began to fall, the stain spreading on her shirt. They seemed frozen in a film still – Nicholas looking back, the girl falling – then a smoke bomb was thrown, the militia, through the barricade, were joined by others running up from the beach. It was impossible to make out what was happening and impossible to take one's eyes from the screen.

Then the television blacked out. Mrs Forrester covered her face with her hands. Mary watched the blank screen, dry-eyed. Her waiter crouched by the set, fiddled delicately with the controls, checked the fuse in the plug and then turned to face them with a shrug that said, 'There you are, it is the same for all of us. Victims of the force of circumstance.' He sighed his regret and left the room with a little bow from the neck.

Much later that night Mary found the parcel Cross had given her, still on the bed where she had left it. About to toss it aside, she opened it after all. The icon blazed. At last she could weep.

Part Four

15

The deckchairs outside the Tea Room bellied their canvases in the breeze. There was a spit of rain in the grey sky. Tomorrow it might be as sunny as ever but this was a warning: the summer had ended.

This had been the most recurrent of all Mary's dreams of the place – a resort out of season. A newspaper blew along the beach and they had the promenade to themselves, except for an advancing figure, with stomach sailing before and one hand to his Panama, the other for his stick. Count Dobi inclined his head, very correct, as a superior might acknowledge the presence of lesser mortals.

At the start of the emergency the knitting ladies had vanished from the lobby and now would not return, bearing away with them their whispers and their sighs to winter quarters. There was cloud over the mountains most days. Indoors – as in every southern country that endures wintry weather but refuses to acknowledge it – shutters banged, windows rattled, there were draughts, not a stick of comfortable furniture. With difficulty Mary had managed to get extra blankets.

The palms were tattered after last night's gale. Nicholas paused, his hand on the railing, and looked out to sea.

'Who was that?'

'Dobi. Count Dobi – you remember? Or perhaps you never met him. Gives me the creeps.'

Nicholas nodded but had already lost interest. His attention span was still short. Over the last fortnight he had more or less mended physically but his mind seemed turned away from Mary, inward, fixed upon some landscape she could only dimly imagine. She had expected this, had been forewarned;

but there was more: a feeling that through the time of their separation something had happened to their marriage – as though it had a life of its own and might undergo an independent metamorphosis, beyond their control.

Absurd. Mary pulled on her headscarf and ran after Nicholas.

'I wish we could go home.' She wanted to take his arm, but held back.

He was emphatic. 'We can't leave Gwendell.'

'No. No, of course not.'

'And she can't fly after a stroke as bad as that.'

Mary shook her head in agreement. They turned away from the sea, inland, towards the hospital on the edge of town. She had to walk fast to keep up with him, he was every day so anxious to get to Gwendell's bedside, only there seemed to find any kind of peace.

In the same way, the night of their rescue, when Mary first saw them in one room at the hospital – the accident reception – she had noticed how the released hostages clung together, shy of those from whom they had parted. Simon Forrester cried when he saw his mother, but it was Nancy Prewitt's hand he wanted to hold. All were talking with concern of the terrorists, one of whom had been killed in the militia attack, two dangerously injured. Their faces were smoke-smeared and their eyes manically bright. Mary was allowed only five minutes with Nicholas before a nun clucked her away, and he had appeared almost thankful to see her go, as if her presence asked too much of him. In the police car on the way back to the Pension, Mary and Rosa had not talked. Mrs Forrester plucked at the material of her skirt. 'Simon hardly seemed to know me,' she said, 'but the doctor told me that is natural, we must expect it. It will be quite a long time perhaps. We must be satisfied they are free and alive. He spoke English. Do you think the doctors here are good?'

That night, after the shooting, the confusion, the rescue, when it was all over and they were safe, Gwendell had a severe stroke that paralysed her entirely down the left side of her body.

When Nicholas asked her, Mary said of course she understood, someone must stay. Simon was too ill, Rosa had already been away too long, keeping Mary company, and Nancy – even if she were fit enough – would drive Gwendell mad. Of them all, Nicholas was in the best shape so he must stay, and Mary with him. At the airport they waved off Nancy and Simon, the Forresters, Manzarotti, Rosa and Joe. All but Simon had made depositions to the police. They might be asked to return to give evidence if the two remaining terrorists survived, but the authorities gave the impression that they would be glad if the matter resolved itself. The Germans were asking daily for the extradition of Helga Langer. She was wanted in Italy too, as was the Arab. 'They're not too frightfully keen on extradition here,' Peter Piper explained. 'On the other hand, those two are an embarrassment they could do without now.' Everyone knew what he meant by now. A Soviet submarine had surfaced a few miles offshore.

Rosa had hugged Mary. 'I'll see Chrissie and the infant. Hold on,' she said in a fierce whisper, 'up the school!'

Gwendell woke from a snoring sleep and opened one eye. 'Never thought,' she mumbled, 'I'd get me to a nunnery. Silly old thing.' She closed her eyes again. Nicholas held her hand and, when she woke once more, talked to her gently, gave her water from the feeding-cup.

At first Mary had felt horror and pity for Gwendell, and for herself a sense of being useless, excluded. But over the last week, as the old woman had struggled first for movement, then for speech, and today finally achieved her first coherent words, she had found herself sharing Nicholas's triumph. They were like parents whose child had formed its first sentence.

They walked down the stairs and along the white stone corridors of the converted convent. There was calm and a quiet broken only by a sibilance: the voices of people they could not see, speaking softly. Mary checked the corridor was empty and put her ear to the wall – the whispers were louder here, like an unseen river, but still garbled. For her this had been a country of secret voices, but these were kinder, they seemed to bless. Then there was a glimpse of a green quadrangle through an arched window and a flutter of nuns hurrying without running to cross it; the breeze tweaked at their wimples and they ducked their heads and clutched at their white-winged headgear like girls at the seaside on a windy day.

Nick too had seen it. He smiled, pecked Mary's cheek.

At the reception desk he paused, as he did every day, to ask the condition of the terrorists. When he caught up with Mary he was less buoyant.

'Helga's in a coma.'

Mary nodded and bit her lip. She had never liked this – the terrorists in the same hospital as their victim – but understood that the nursing facilities in the prison hospital were minimal. Later, over dinner, she put down her knife and fork. They were the only diners now, though Peter Piper sometimes joined them.

'I don't see why you care what happens to them. They might have killed you.' The doctors had warned her not to probe, but not to ask would have seemed absurd.

Nicholas shook his head. When he first came out he was big-boned as ever but had lost the bulk that was right for him, so that his clothes appeared too large, hung on over-wide hangers. He had put on flesh now and his sandy hair disguised the grey.

She pressed, gently. 'They *did* kill Waldemar. And Henri.'

He took her hands across the table. 'I can't explain and you'd never understand unless you'd been there.'

'Perhaps I do understand,' she said quietly, thinking of Cross.

'You see,' he went on. 'I think we were all being used in one way or another. Them and us.'

Mary snapped off a bunch of grapes, dunked it in the water bowl. 'The good committee chairman. Sees both sides of the question. You haven't changed.'

He shook his head again, took one of his thin black cigars but sat with it unlit as he struggled to convey his meaning.

'No. It was this crazy feeling all of us had sometime. Almost of comradeship. I know they always say that happens, but actually to experience it . . .' He fumbled for his lighter. 'Perhaps it was the coup while we were in there, the fighting – we shared a common danger. But, besides that, we got to know them as individuals – we had no choice – and few individuals are fiends incarnate all the time. Something wrong with the world had created the situation. They were victims too.'

Mary sighed.

At night his restless sleep disturbed her. He had a horror, she knew, of waking and finding himself alone in the dark. Since Nicholas would never wake her, Mary had learned to sleep lightly, taking daytime naps to make this possible. She became eerily tuned to his night fears. Only then, like a child struggling out of nightmare, would he allow her to hold him. It was on one of these occasions that she gave him the amber. He smiled, and fell asleep with the consoling beads of magical property twined in his fingers.

Sometimes she felt the need for other company and dared not seek Cross's, so she looked up gratefully when a shadow fell across her pad.

'I thought perhaps you would like a stroll? But I mustn't interrupt your writing.' Peter Piper blushed. Mary flipped the pad shut.

'No, really, I wasn't writing. Just sketching – but not for public consumption. I do that when I can't write. I'd love a walk. Where shall we go? To the beach?'

'Actually there's a rather interesting cemetery, if you haven't seen it?'

'No, I haven't. I'll just leave a message for Nick. He's at the hospital. I said I'd join him later.'

'Ah, yes.'

Mary left her note, pushed her sketch pad in her bag and joined Piper. It was sunny today and the mid-afternoon sun could still burn. Piper wore the type of floppy white sun-hat well-brought up children at pre-war Frinton might have sported. His stride was jerky but resolute as he led the way uphill, along a dirt track through parched grass where cicadas still chattered drily. A solemn weaving file of ants crossed their path. Mary wished she too had brought a hat.

'And how is Dame Gwendoline?'

'Well, much better. But there's always the risk of another stroke. At her age, you know. It's so awful, it's the same as poor Waldemar.'

'Indeed.'

At the top of the hill no wall protected the wind-blown cemetery, only the archway remained. *Hic locus terribilis est et porta caeli*. Mary fingered the crumbling inscription.

'My Latin's not up to much.'

'Ah yes. I believe it means something like: this is a terrible place and the gate of heaven. Rather like life, I suppose, in a way. They are the words used when a Cathedral's consecrated, I gather. Not that there was anything of that sort here.'

There was a white-washed chapel. Sea grasses and flowers grew among the graves. There were the photographs and little tokens one finds in such places, some vulgar, all touching. A marble angel faced the sea, arms spread to embrace the sky. Mary followed Peter Piper round to the back of the chapel and into a small walled graveyard – a surprise. Here, all was immaculately tended, the gravestones simpler, the flowers fresher. Pale butterflies danced among the grasses. Piper sat, puffing, on a stone seat and fanned his face with his hat. Mary sat beside him.

'The English cemetery,' he said. 'Funny. They're all over the place, you know. All those ninteenth-century travellers who never got home.'

Mary remembered the writing-room in the Pension du Parc. 'It's beautifully looked after.'

'One does what one can, you know.'

'You?'

'I like it up here.'

Mary smiled as she thought of Piper weeding and watering his little England. The air was scented with lavender, rosemary and late honeysuckle. A bee bumbled and browsed among the lavender.

Mary sat with her eyes half-closed, the sun on her lids, and heard Piper say, 'Pity about Hugo Cross.'

'Cross?' She was startled, wide awake. Whatever it was that Piper had to say, Mary knew that he had brought her up here to tell her.

'Done a bunk. I'm afraid they found, you see, he was serving two masters. Double agent.'

Mary let out a breath. 'Thank you for telling me.' She thought perhaps she knew already. She stared at the English gravestones, not seeing, thinking: this is his punishment and mine. We live, after all, in a moral universe. 'Do they know where he's gone?'

'Over there, I expect.' Piper pulled his nose in the familiar gesture of embarrassment. She was extraordinarily touched that he had bothered and that he had done it this way. She stood and walked without purpose among the graves, stooping to read the names and touch the flowers. She called back, 'These roses – what are they?'

Mary had released him from his shyness in the face of catastrophe. Piper scuttled over. 'Old-fashioned. Not much colour but the best for scent.'

'They're lovely.'

Below them, the bells of the city called the end of siesta.

'I'm due at the hospital.'

They picked their way down the hill, Mary broke the silence. 'You'll be going home soon?'

For the first time Piper looked straight at her. He gave her his odd little smile. 'Home? I daresay. Yes, it would be good to go home.'

He delivered her to the hospital by taxi. Mary stooped to call goodbye, then the door was slammed and she stood for a moment on the hospital steps, watching as they drew away. Life. She imagined Piper sitting it out in that small garden of the dead.

Gwendell had become their talisman. Though neither spoke of it, nor had entirely formulated the idea even in their minds,

Mary and Nicholas wondered sometimes if Gwendell were to recover, their marriage might mend.

Today, after the visit to the cemetery, Mary found Nicholas waiting impatiently for her outside Gwendell's room.

'Where were you? I've been here an hour.'

'I left a message.'

'She had a relapse.'

Mary was dazed, still shocked from the news Piper had given her, and now this. It was cool and shadowed here – blinded from the sun, she could hardly make out Nick's face. Her own cheeks held the warmth of the afternoon in the open air.

An orderly – not a nun – was sitting by Gwendell's bed. With her cheeks as red as though she'd pinched them, her broad smile and capable forearms, she reminded Mary of the scrubbing woman at the Pension. She indicated that she would leave for a moment and pointed to the bell they were to ring, in emergency presumably, or when they left.

Gwendell was propped in a sitting position, eyes shut, breathing with a terrible rasping. Across the bed, Mary said, 'Another stroke?'

Nicholas shook his head. 'Bronchitis.'

'What's that horrible thing round her neck?'

'A collar to keep her head up.'

Mary shuddered. 'Can she hear us?'

Nicholas shrugged. 'I don't think so.'

She wouldn't want us to see her like this, Mary thought and, her hands clenched in her lap, let her gaze wander around the room, until it rested on a crucifix. That would be Gwendell's first sight on waking, her last on sleeping. No gentle Jesus this – the figure was carved in a dark wood, the face harsh, the head not tipped to one side but thrusting on corded neck, in agony, as though to wrench the body from the frame.

Mary noticed that Nicholas had not shaved today. He sat heavily on the small hospital chair, his shoulders hunched, his big hands loose between his knees.

'I went for a walk with Peter Piper,' she said. 'You ought to get some air. I could stay here.'

He looked at her as though he were purblind, his eyes sunken.

A nun came and shooshed them away in her little English.

It rained in the night. Mary turned away from the thought of Cross. She put her hand on Nick's shoulder.

'You're not asleep either, are you? D'you want to talk?'

He lay on his back, staring at the ceiling, hands locked behind his head.

'I don't know. I'm frightened. I'm sorry. I wish I could say what it is. All that time we were in danger every minute, yet outside it seems terrifying. It was like being a child there – all the decisions were taken for you. This sounds mad.'

'No.'

'Then there was the fighting, and we didn't know what was going on. When we were freed, I felt like an animal, imprisoned for years, then it won't leave its cage. So now – I need you and there's nothing I can give you.'

Mary said, 'You'd be better away from here.'

They slept at last and this time it was Nick who shook her from a dream. 'You called out.'

'What?'

'Couldn't tell.'

She was soaked with sweat.

'It was nothing. Just a nightmare I have sometimes.'

In the morning the rain had washed the air clean. For a week of sun they hardly noticed the weather, but each day sat by Gwendell. The Russians were threatening still, Piper said – a MIG jet had buzzed a civilian airliner, there were rumblings of a comradely force sent to assist the people in their glorious struggle against over-zealous revisionists. Piper advised the Lambs to leave.

But Mary too could not have abandoned this vigil. The first day Gwendell's breathing improved and she opened her eyes, the next she could take mushy food, the third she could feed herself and demanded her teeth. By the end of the week the collar was gone and she was taking her first steps out of bed. When the Lambs arrived, at the end of her afternoon nap she opened her eyes and said clearly, 'You may go home now. I have no intention of dying. If I change my mind, I daresay I can manage alone.'

Nicholas and Mary smiled – Mary kissed Gwendell's cheek, kissed Nicholas, laughing, almost crying. She felt absurdly proud.

Gwendell became a tyrant, demanding books, spectacles, conversation, scarves, handkerchiefs, shawls, mirrors, sweets. Having dismissed them, she wouldn't let them go, until Mary said, 'We have to leave in a few days, I'm afraid. Apart from anything else, we pay our own bills at the Pension now.'

'But that's an outrage! The Congress –'

'When the Congress collapsed the organising committee in Brussels disbanded itself.'

Gwendell snorted.

'Anyway,' Mary said, 'the consul's wife is flying home sometime in the next couple of weeks. She's happy to go with you whenever you are strong enough. She's very sensible.'

'Sensible? I don't need that. I can be sensible for two. Is she clever? And smart? Can't stand stupid women. Now go away. I want to sleep.'

Leaving, Mary looked out of the window and realised for the first time that the hospital stood on the cliff above the hoop-shaped beach where she and Rosa had snatched those odd few hours of innocence. She took Nicholas's arm and they ran down the stairs and into the street.

'Let's go out for dinner tonight,' he said.

The town was tense still and although with fewer incidents the curfew had been lifted, there was little choice of restaurants. Some had gone in the fighting, others, with no tourists to serve, stayed closed after the crisis.

So, of all places, it was at the Metropole they finished, sitting not in the vast dining-room but at one of the tables set out on the very balcony where Mary and Cross had talked at the opening of the Congress and, more recently, she had seen Blok speak to the jubilant crowd. From the shrubbery below there was the scent she remembered of some sweet decay.

But the tablecloths were spotless and each had a centre-piece of the everlasting carnations. Mary smiled. 'They always seem to be in season, don't they. I've never liked them much.'

She felt shy with Nicholas tonight. At the next table a young man reached across and whispered to his girl, holding the tips of her fingers in his. By the pink-shaded lamp Mary could see that his hands were perfectly manicured, his cuffs white and a little too long, while his neat, shining black hair was too slick and short for modern fashions. The girl, murmuring back, lowered her lids and curved her coral mouth into a demure and teasing smile. Both, Mary thought, belonged to another age, as did the hotel, crumbling even more after the recent battles, an ageing beauty who should only be seen at night.

Nicholas followed her discreet gaze. 'Amazing, isn't it.'

'Love?'

'That she should fancy such a lizard,' he said drily. But he touched Mary's cheek and with his finger gently traced the jagged line of her scar, faded now to purplish-white and under make-up hardly visible, though she would never lose it. 'Whatever's this?'

'I got kicked in the face. My own fault. Running round town after the first fighting.' Looking for Hugo Cross, she reflected. Will I ever tell Nick? Probably not. It has nothing to do with us now.

Nick was appalled; for the first time since his release he seemed really to see her, to listen to her words. He's getting better, Mary reflected, watching him talk. He'll slip back into that other, terrifying world, but he'll return to himself, to me. She took a sip of the wine.

'Mmn. French. What wild delight.' She said idly, 'D'you think people change?'

He pondered. The same Nick – still that neat little pause while he weighed a question.

'I think different aspects of their personalities emerge.' He smiled. 'I can never quite think of Nancy as Poor Prewitt any more. Why d'you ask?'

Mary emptied her glass. She shrugged. 'Nothing really. I just haven't liked myself very much lately. Perhaps everyone thinks they're rather nice until they discover otherwise. I suppose some never do discover. The knack may be to live with one's monsters.'

'Come on, monster. Bedtime.'

Mary had to wear a shawl to walk in the evenings now. It was the blue time of night, soft, a wash of tender violet drawn over everything: faces, dresses, sky, sea, stone. Nicholas still tired easily. They rested, leaning on the balustrade along the promenade, not far from the boarded-up Tea Room.

'Does that place worry you?'

'Not tonight.'

'I wonder if there'll be a letter from Chrissie tomorrow. Grandparents! I hadn't thought of that.' Mary put her arm through Nick's. She pondered. 'This has all been so strange – as if we'd strayed into a mad world. And yet for the time we were in it, it was the only real one.' It's still there, she thought, we might step into it again, any day. They walked on. 'D'you know, Rosa swears Joe's CIA? That clown. It's so crazy it's probably true.' The thought came to her then: could it have been Joe who tipped someone off about Cross? The revelation – for she felt sure, abruptly, that it was the truth – made her stumble. Nick caught her elbow.

They were at the Pension door. It was a stranger behind the desk who handed them the key.

They still did not make love, but they lay in each other's arms and Mary's sleep was dreamless that night.

16

There were days still of wild effulgent beauty, boiling gold, so theatrical that Mary would pause in the midst of their preparations to leave. She stood at the window with Cross's kaftan in her hands, held the material for a moment to her lips, traced the pattern the birds wove in the tissue-like fabric. Then decisively, before she could give the matter further thought, carried it downstairs past the stranger at the lobby desk, to the kitchen quarters. The kitchen was empty and there was no one, either, in the yard. Mary paused, wondered if this were the same yard she had seen from Joe Porterhouse's room, but looking up could see no grilled window, only wall, ivy-covered. And yet it must have been this yard. She shook her head – certainties, even within the layout of the Pension, were shifting, escaping her – went back into the kitchen and laid the folded kaftan on the table. Mary imagined the scrubbing-woman finding it, holding it up to herself and grinning gap-toothed; the girl in the red scarf receiving it, touching it in wonder. Would she dance in it?

The icon – that was more difficult, for she could neither keep it nor entirely give it away. Perhaps save it for Chrissie's son? Cross had explained to her that for the iconographer each colour and configuration had a symbolic significance which was immutable. Superstitiously, Mary felt that for Cross's sake she must keep the icon safe. She wrapped it again, carefully, and laid it at the bottom of her case.

Nick telephoned. Mary took a cab to the hospital. They stood in the cloister, cold, out of the sun.

'I was packing.' Mary kept her voice low, nuns passed, smiled, bustled, or, catching the violence of her tone, ran, their holy boots invisible. 'Do you *realise* that I thought Gwendell was dead? You got me here and it's that German bitch.'

He looked chilled. She went on like a mad woman, railing.

'I'm glad. They killed Waldemar and Henri. Have you forgotten they killed Waldemar? That we shall be flying back tomorrow with his ashes in the hold? I could have killed her myself.'

'Stop,' he said. 'So much violence already. So much to come.'

'Now I'm here I want to see her. To see that she's dead.'

'That's horrible.'

'No.' Mary shook her head, calmer now. 'I just want to be sure that it's finished.'

Nicholas looked at her gently, solemnly. 'It'll never be finished now.'

All Mary thought when she did see the body of Helga Langer was that she seemed very young.

The day they left, the Pension was closing for the season. They were served their breakfast in the lobby.

'Oh, I've only just noticed,' Mary said, 'the carnation seller's gone.'

The town, like the Pension, had a barred and bolted look against the winter, or the Russians. At the airport a thin rain was falling. Mary shivered, caught Nicholas's sleeve and ran up the steps.

Over the Adriatic the sky cleared and there was Italy and poor sweet Venice sinking in her golden bath. The higher they flew, the simpler and more beautiful the earth appeared.

FICTION

GENERAL

☐ Chains	Justin Adams	£1.25
☐ Secrets	F. Lee Bailey	£1.25
☐ Skyship	John Brosnan	£1.65
☐ The Free Fishers	John Buchan	£1.50
☐ Huntingtower	John Buchan	£1.50
☐ Midwinter	John Buchan	£1.25
☐ A Prince of the Captivity	John Buchan	£1.25
☐ The Eve of St Venus	Anthony Burgess	£1.10
☐ Nothing Like the Sun	Anthony Burgess	£1.50
☐ The Memoirs of Maria Brown	John Cleland	£1.25
☐ The Last Liberator	John Clive	£1.25
☐ Wyndward Fury	Norman Daniels	£1.50
☐ Ladies in Waiting	Gwen Davis	£1.50
☐ The Money Wolves	Paul Erikson	£1.50
☐ Rich Little Poor Girl	Terence Feely	£1.50
☐ Fever Pitch	Betty Ferm	£1.50
☐ The Bride of Lowther Fell	Margaret Forster	£1.75
☐ Forced Feedings	Maxine Herman	£1.50
☐ Savannah Blue	William Harrison	£1.50
☐ Duncton Wood	William Horwood	£1.95
☐ Dingley Falls	Michael Malone	£1.95
☐ Gossip	Marc Olden	£1.25
☐ Buccaneer	Dudley Pope	£1.50
☐ An Inch of Fortune	Simon Raven	£1.25
☐ The Dream Makers	John Sherlock	£1.50
☐ The Reichling Affair	Jack Stoneley	£1.75
☐ Eclipse	Margaret Tabor	£1.35
☐ Pillars of the Establishment	Alexander Thynn	£1.50
☐ Cat Stories	Stella Whitelaw	£1.10

WESTERN — BLADE SERIES by Matt Chisholm

☐ No. 5 The Colorado Virgins	85p
☐ No. 6 The Mexican Proposition	85p
☐ No. 7 The Arizona Climax	85p
☐ No. 8 The Nevada Mustang	85p
☐ No. 9 The Montana Deadlock	95p
☐ No. 10 The Cheyenne Trap	95p
☐ No. 11 The Navaho Trail	95p
☐ No. 12 The Last Act	95p

WESTERN — McALLISTER SERIES by Matt Chisholm

☐ McAllister and the Spanish Gold	95p
☐ McAllister on the Commanche Crossing	95p
☐ McAllister Never Surrenders	95p
☐ McAllister and the Cheyenne Trap	95p

SCIENCE FICTION

☐ Times Without Number	John Brunner	£1.10
☐ The Dancers of Arun	Elizabeth A. Lynn	£1.50
☐ Watchtower	Elizabeth A. Lynn	£1.10

WAR

☐ The Andersen Assault	Peter Leslie	£1.25
☐ Killers under a Cruel Sky	Peter Leslie	£1.25
☐ The Serbian Triangle	Peter Saunders	£1.10
☐ Jenny's War	Jack Stoneley	£1.25

NON-FICTION

GENERAL

☐ The Chinese Mafia	Fenton Bresler	£1.50
☐ The Piracy Business	Barbara Conway	£1.50
☐ Strange Deaths	John Dunning	£1.35
☐ Shocktrauma	John Franklin & Alan Doelp	£1.50
☐ The War Machine	James Avery Joyce	£1.50

BIOGRAPHY/AUTOBIOGRAPHY

☐ All You Needed Was Love	John Blake	£1.50
☐ Clues to the Unknown	Robert Cracknell	£1.50
☐ William Wordsworth	Hunter Davies	£1.95
☐ The Family Story	Lord Denning	£1.95
☐ The Borgias	Harry Edgington	£1.50
☐ Rachman	Shirley Green	£1.50
☐ Nancy Astor	John Grigg	£2.95
☐ Monty: The Making of a General 1887-1942	Nigel Hamilton	£4.95
☐ The Windsors in Exile	Michael Pye	£1.50
☐ 50 Years with Mountbatten	Charles Smith	£1.25
☐ Maria Callas	Arianna Stassinopoulos	£1.75
☐ Swanson on Swanson	Gloria Swanson	£2.50

HEALTH/SELF-HELP

☐ The Hamlyn Family First Aid Book	Dr Robert Andrew	£1.50
☐ Girl!	Brandenburger & Curry	£1.25
☐ The Good Health Guide for Women	Cooke & Dworkin	£2.95
☐ The Babysitter Book	Curry & Cunningham	£1.25
☐ Living Together	Dyer & Berlins	£1.50
☐ The Pick of Woman's Own Diets	Jo Foley	95p
☐ Coping With Redundancy	Fred Kemp	£1.50
☐ Cystitis: A Complete Self-help Guide	Angela Kilmartin	£1.00
☐ Fit for Life	Donald Norfolk	£1.35
☐ The Stress Factor	Donald Norfolk	£1.25
☐ Fat is a Feminist Issue	Susie Orbach	£1.25
☐ Fat is a Feminist Issue II	Susie Orbach	£3.50
☐ Living With Your New Baby	Rakowitz & Rubin	£1.50
☐ Related to Sex	Claire Rayner	£1.50
☐ Natural Sex	Mary Shivanandan	£1.25
☐ Woman's Own Birth Control	Dr Michael Smith	£1.25
☐ Overcoming Depression	Dr Andrew Stanway	£1.50
☐ Health Shock	Martin Weitz	£1.75

POCKET HEALTH GUIDES

☐ Depression and Anxiety	Dr Arthur Graham	85p
☐ Diabetes	Dr Alex D. G. Gunn	85p
☐ Heart Trouble	Dr Simon Joseph	85p
☐ High Blood Pressure	Dr James Knapton	85p
☐ The Menopause	Studd & Thom	85p
☐ Children's Illnesses	Dr Luke Zander	85p

TRAVEL

☐ The Complete Traveller	Joan Bakewell	£1.95
☐ Time Out London Shopping Guide	Lindsey Bareham	£1.50
☐ A Walk Around the Lakes	Hunter Davies	£1.75
☐ Britain By Train	Patrick Goldring	£1.75
☐ England By Bus	Elizabeth Gundrey	£1.25
☐ Staying Off the Beaten Track	Elizabeth Gundrey	£2.95
☐ Britain at Your Feet	Wickers & Pedersen	£1.75

HUMOUR

☐ Don't Quote Me	Atyeo & Green	£1.00
☐ Ireland Strikes Back!	Seamus B. Gorrah	85p
☐ Pun Fun	Paul Jennings	95p
☐ 1001 Logical Laws	John Peers	95p
☐ The Devil's Bedside Book	Leonard Rossiter	85p

FICTION

CRIME/ADVENTURE/SUSPENSE

☐ The Killing In The Market	John Ball with Bevan Smith	£1.00
☐ In the Heat of the Night	John Ball	£1.00
☐ Johnny Get Your Gun	John Ball	£1.00
☐ The Cool Cottontail	John Ball	£1.00
☐ The Megawind Cancellation	Bernard Boucher	£1.25
☐ Tunnel	Hal Friedman	£1.35
☐ Tagget	Irving A. Greenfield	£1.25
☐ Don't be no Hero	Leonard Harris	£1.25
☐ The Blunderer	Patricia Highsmith	£1.25
☐ A Game for the Living	Patricia Highsmith	£1.25
☐ Those Who Walk Away	Patricia Highsmith	£1.25
☐ The Tremor of Forgery	Patricia Highsmith	£1.25
☐ The Two Faces of January	Patricia Highsmith	£1.25
☐ Labyrinth	Eric Mackenzie-Lamb	£1.25
☐ The Hunted	Elmore Leonard	£1.25
☐ The Traitor Machine	Max Marquis	£1.25
☐ The Triad Imperative	Dwight Martin	£1.50
☐ Confess, Fletch	Gregory Mcdonald	90p
☐ Fletch	Gregory Mcdonald	90p
☐ Fletch's Fortune	Gregory Mcdonald	£1.25
☐ Flynn	Gregory Mcdonald	95p
☐ All the Queen's Men	Guiy de Montfort	£1.25
☐ Pandora Man	Newcomb & Schaefer	£1.25
☐ Skyfire	Thomas Page	£1.50
☐ The Last Prisoner	James Robson	£1.50
☐ The Croesus Conspiracy	Ben Stein	£1.25
☐ Deadline in Jakarta	Ian Stewart	£1.25
☐ The Seizing of Singapore	Ian Stewart	£1.00
☐ The Earhart Betrayal	James Stewart Thayer	£1.50

HISTORICAL ROMANCE/ROMANCE/SAGA

☐ Hawksmoor	Aileen Armitage	£1.75
☐ Pipistrelle	Aileen Armitage	£1.25
☐ Blaze of Passion	Stephanie Blake	£1.25
☐ Daughter of Destiny	Stephanie Blake	£1.50
☐ Flowers of Fire	Stephanie Blake	£1.50
☐ So Wicked My Desire	Stephanie Blake	£1.50
☐ Unholy Desires	Stephanie Blake	£1.50
☐ Wicked is My Flesh	Stephanie Blake	£1.50
☐ Lovers and Dancers	Michael Feeney Callan	£1.50
☐ The Far Morning	Brenda Clarke	£1.50
☐ The Lofty Banners	Brenda Clarke	£1.75
☐ Night at Sea Abbey	Virginia Coffman	£1.00
☐ The Blacksmith	Louise Cooper	£1.25
☐ My Love, My Land	Judy Gardiner	£1.25
☐ Walburga's Eve	Elizabeth Hann	£1.35
☐ The Opera Dancer	Sandra Heath	£1.50
☐ The Rebel Heart	Anna James	£1.25
☐ Fires of Winter	Johanna Lindsey	£1.50
☐ A Pirate's Love	Johanna Lindsey	£1.25
☐ Trade Imperial	Alan Lloyd	£1.35
☐ Dance Barefoot	Margaret Maddocks	95p
☐ The Open Door	Margaret Maddocks	£1.25
☐ The Open Door	Margaret Maddocks	£1.25
☐ All We Know of Heaven	Dore Mullen	£1.25
☐ The Far Side of Destiny	Dore Mullen	£1.50
☐ New Year's Eve	Jeannie Sakol	£1.50
☐ The Pride	Judith Saxton	£1.50
☐ Kingdom's Castle	Daoma Winston	£1.00
☐ Shadow of an Unknown Woman	Daoma Winston	£1.00
☐ Skeleton Key	Daoma Winston	95p

REFERENCE

☐ **The Sunday Times Guide to Movies on Television**	Angela & Elkan Allan	£1.50
☐ **The Cheiro Book of Fate and Fortune**		£1.50
☐ **Hunter Davies's Book of British Lists**		£1.25
☐ **NME Guide to Rock Cinema**	Fred Dellar	£1.50
☐ **What's Wrong With Your Pet?**	Hugo Kerr	95p
☐ **The Drinker's Companion**	Derek Nimmo	£1.25
☐ **The Complete Book of Cleaning**	Barty Phillips	£1.50
☐ **The Oscar Movies from A-Z**	Roy Pickard	£1.25
☐ **Collecting For Profit**	Sam Richards	£1.25
☐ **Islam**	D. S. Roberts	£1.50
☐ **Questions of Motoring Law**	John Spencer	£1.25
☐ **Questions of Law**	Bill Thomas	£1.25

GAMES AND PASTIMES

☐ **The Hamlyn Book of Wordways 1**		75p
☐ **The Hamlyn Family Quiz Book**		85p

WAR

☐ **The Battle of Malta**	Joseph Attard	£1.50
☐ **World War 3**	Edited by Shelford Bidwell	£1.50
☐ **The Black Angels**	Rupert Butler	£1.35
☐ **Gestapo**	Rupert Butler	£1.50
☐ **Hand of Steel**	Rupert Butler	£1.35
☐ **The Flight of the Mew Gull**	Alex Henshaw	£1.75
☐ **Sigh for a Merlin**	Alex Henshaw	£1.50
☐ **Hitler's Secret Life**	Glenn B. Infield	£1.25

GARDENING

☐ **'Jock' Davidson's House Plant Book**		£1.50
☐ **A Vegetable Plot for Two — or More**	D. B. Clay Jones	£1.00
☐ **Salads the Year Round**	Joy Larkcom	£1.50
☐ **Gardening Tips of A Lifetime**	Fred Loads	£1.50
☐ **Sunday Telegraph Patio Gardening**	Robert Pearson	£1.00
☐ **Greenhouse Gardening**	Sue Phillips	£1.25

COOKERY

☐ **A-Z of Health Foods**	Carol Bowen	£1.50
☐ **The Giant Sandwich Book**	Carol Bowen	£1.50
☐ **Vegetarian Cookbook**	Dave Dutton	£1.50
☐ **Jewish Cookbook**	Florence Greenberg	£1.50
☐ **Know Your Onions**	Kate Hastrop	95p
☐ **Indian Cooking**	Attia Hosain and Sita Pasricha	£1.50
☐ **Home Preserving and Bottling**	Gladys Mann	80p
☐ **Home Baked Breads & Cakes**	Mary Norwak	75p
☐ **Easy Icing**	Marguerite Patten	85p
☐ **Wine Making At Home**	Francis Pinnegar	80p
☐ **Cooking for Christmas**	Shona Crawford Poole	£1.50
☐ **Microwave Cookbook**	Jill Spencer	£1.25
☐ **Mixer and Blender Cookbook**	Myra Street	80p
☐ **Diabetic Cookbook**	Elisabeth Russell Taylor	£1.50
☐ **The Hamlyn Pressure Cookbook**	Jane Todd	85p

HUMOUR

☐ **Don't Quote Me**	Atyeo & Green	£1.00
☐ **Ireland Strikes Back!**	Seamus B. Gorrah	85p
☐ **Pun Fun**	Paul Jennings	95p
☐ **1001 Logical Laws**	John Peers	95p
☐ **The Devil's Bedside Book**	Leonard Rossiter	85p